"Annette Blair has the magic . . . taining joie de vivre parano . . . The mystery is cleverly const . . .

"A fast-paced, fascinating ad . . . series . . . A book by Annet . . . coaster ride, and *Death by Diamonds* is no exception!"
—*Fresh Fiction*

"It was fabulous—the best Vintage Magic Mystery yet. Full of magic, mystery, and classic Blair style. Maddie's antics are always fun to read, and the hint of romance is a teasing heat that leaves you wondering and wanting more."
—*Fang-tastic Books*

"To say Annette Blair has revved up the drama and intensity would be putting it too mildly . . . One of the most interesting mysteries I have read this year. A magnificent story!"
—*Huntress Reviews*

"An exciting, humorous roller-coaster ride . . . I cannot recommend Annette Blair's books enough, and this one is no exception to that. It already has a place on my keeper shelf."
—*ParaNormal Romance*

Larceny and Lace

"Another fast-paced novel that keeps the reader entertained from the word go! Annette Blair's characters are warm and endearing, and you feel as if you're . . . . ds among the p . . . . utler family a . . . . thor."
—*Fresh Fiction*

A Veiled Deception

SKIRTING
the Grave

ANNETTE BLAIR

BERKLEY PRIME CRIME, NEW YORK

THE BERKLEY PUBLISHING GROUP
Published by the Penguin Group
Penguin Group (USA) Inc.
375 Hudson Street, New York, New York 10014, USA

Penguin Group (Canada), 90 Eglinton Avenue East, Suite 700, Toronto, Ontario M4P 2Y3, Canada
(a division of Pearson Penguin Canada Inc.)
Penguin Books Ltd., 80 Strand, London WC2R 0RL, England
Penguin Group Ireland, 25 St. Stephen's Green, Dublin 2, Ireland (a division of Penguin Books Ltd.)
Penguin Group (Australia), 250 Camberwell Road, Camberwell, Victoria 3124, Australia
(a division of Pearson Australia Group Pty. Ltd.)
Penguin Books India Pvt. Ltd., 11 Community Centre, Panchsheel Park, New Delhi—110 017, India
Penguin Group (NZ), 67 Apollo Drive, Rosedale, Auckland 0632, New Zealand
(a division of Pearson New Zealand Ltd.)
Penguin Books (South Africa) (Pty.) Ltd., 24 Sturdee Avenue, Rosebank, Johannesburg 2196,
South Africa

Penguin Books Ltd., Registered Offices: 80 Strand, London WC2R 0RL, England

This is a work of fiction. Names, characters, places, and incidents either are the product of the author's imagination or are used fictitiously, and any resemblance to actual persons, living or dead, business establishments, events, or locales is entirely coincidental. The publisher does not have any control over and does not assume any responsibility for author or third-party websites or their content.

SKIRTING THE GRAVE

A Berkley Prime Crime Book / published by arrangement with the author

PRINTING HISTORY
Berkley Prime Crime mass-market edition / July 2011

Copyright © 2011 by Annette Blair.
Excerpt from *Cloaked in Malice* by Annette Blair copyright © by Annette Blair.
Cover illustration by Kimberly Schamber.
Cover design by Rita Frangie.
Interior text design by Laura K. Corless.

ISBN: 978-0-425-24222-3

BERKLEY® PRIME CRIME
Berkley Prime Crime Books are published by The Berkley Publishing Group,
a division of Penguin Group (USA) Inc.,
375 Hudson Street, New York, New York 10014.
BERKLEY® PRIME CRIME and the PRIME CRIME logo are trademarks of Penguin Group (USA) Inc.

PRINTED IN THE UNITED STATES OF AMERICA

10 9 8 7 6 5 4 3 2 1

This book is dedicated,
with much love, to
Deb Jobert.
Forever friend, great writer.
For mutual support, shared laughter,
awesome conferences.
And for making the early days so special.
Smiles linger.

Author's Note

Historic Mystic, Connecticut, is a treat as is the Mystic River, both well worth a long visit. Mystick Falls, to the north, however, is a figment of my imagination, as are the locations of my characters' homes and of the town's governing body. I have too much respect for the real thing to portray them any other way.

One

She wore a short skirt and a tight sweater and her figure described a set of parabolas that could cause cardiac arrest in a yak.   —WOODY ALLEN, *GETTING EVEN*, 1973

Eve Meyers, my BFF, a gothic fashionista with a steampunk edge, tall in her black and brass Lindi Buckle Leather Booties, invaded my vintage dress shop with mischief aforethought. "Madeira? Did you ever tell Nick about that thermonuclear kiss you shared with Werner the night you and the detective slept together?"

Even though we were alone right now, I grew warm in my fifties Lilli Ann flared-sleeved, cinch-waisted, pencil-skirted suit. I'd purchased it at a miracle of a bargain, though a rabid collector would pay a grand for the set.

You had to love the goods you sold, which I aced, but right now, I wasn't loving my BFF too darn much.

Eve knew she'd hit home when she turned to face my

beverage buffet. "Caffeine. Gotta have more caffeine. My morning fix has left the building." She chose a zinger of a caramel tea as black and powerful as her outfit.

From the back, her long, straight hennaed hair spilled over the stand-up collar of her cotton point textured faille jacket, same fabric as her skintight cropped pants. For contrast, I'd designed it to be worn with that bold-print girlie top—earth tones hidden among the black—a barely there ruffle flowing just below the cropped waist of her jacket.

Her necklace of assorted copper gears picked up the red sheen from her hair, which she flipped as she turned back to me. "If you didn't tell Nick," she said, "you're about to have your chance. I hear he's on his way home." She sipped her tea and eyed me with calculation over the rim of a blue Wedgwood teacup.

"Werner and I did *not* sleep together!" I snapped. "We were out cold, both of us concussed . . . in the same bed. There's a difference."

Dropping the subject, I stacked the fifties outfits I'd sold earlier that morning, to be worn at my sister Brandy's costume fund-raiser this coming Saturday night. "Be right back. Have to top my list of alterations with this lot."

Eve leaned on the doorjamb at the base of my enclosed stairway sipping and watching as I climbed. "If I didn't know better," she said, "I'd think you're ignoring me."

What I chose to ignore, I acknowledged to myself, was the amusement in her voice. I hung the items to be altered in my work corner, boxed in by several antique sewing machines and a few of today's finest technical wonders that did everything but wear the clothes.

Back downstairs in my sales area, I switched out winter purses for summer box bags in straws, metallics, Bakelite, and Lucite, and showcased their funky shapes: rectangle, trapezoid, beehive, hatbox, lunch box, not to mention the fifties icon: the sleek single-clasp, rectangular box clutch, a purse known to endow its owner with ladylike behavior.

"You and Werner can't escape your scorching past," Eve warned, arms crossed, eyes bright, smile at half-mast. "Neither can you escape me."

Atop the purse pyramid, I placed a white oval Lucite Llewellyn bag, the bottom edged with a two-inch, molded, silver floral band. "Gorgeous," I said.

"Face it," Eve persisted, "the kiss *did* happen. You and Werner couldn't *both* have dreamed it. Besides, *he's* the one who called it 'thermonuclear.'"

"Get out, Meyers!"

Eve's grin grew. "You *didn't* tell Nick, did you?"

I huffed. "First I said I didn't want to talk about it. Then when I tried, Nick didn't want to hear it. So first we avoided the subject and then we avoided each other. Fact is, Nick's been on one secret assignment or another for nearly the entire four months since."

Eve waved a hand. "Excuses, excuses."

"No, seriously, the FBI takes advantage of their special agents that way. Plus we took an official time-out before he left."

"Still, on or off, you and Nick have always stayed friends. What did you do, lose his cell phone number or something?"

I sighed inwardly. "For your amusement, Meyers, I'll admit that Nick seems to have changed his cell phone number."

Before my eyes, she turned into a member of gossip central. "So you *did* try to call him?"

"Of course, I did." Once, after a lonely six-pack of Dos Equis. Bad idea: the call and the beer. Both had come back to haunt me.

"Hah!" Eve did smug well. Probably reading me like a book. "You procrastinated beyond what was reasonable, confession-wise." she said. "Now he's either pouting or plain old steaming."

I turned on the air-conditioning. "Thanks, Sherlock Poppycock. I never would have figured that out."

"Hey." Eve tapped her lips with a finger. "Ever think that maybe *Werner* told Nick about the kiss?"

I raised a brow. "Your optimistic encouragement is underwhelming."

Her watch alarm rang. "Gotta run. If Kyle's metallic gold, stretch Lamborghini is already sitting in my driveway, it's giving my frugal, old-world mother a heart attack."

"I can't believe you're still dating Kyle DeLong. Multibillionaires are so *not* your style."

Eve swallowed, hand on the doorknob. "You're trying to scare me to pay me back. Sure, he's practically a record for me, but he's just a plaything."

"A plaything who's buying a mansion in the town where you live."

"Because having him stay at my house would *kill* my mother, literally."

"Let's hear it for the odd couple," I said.

Kyle's mother, Broadway actress Dominique De-Long, died under suspicious circumstances this winter, and when we went to the city to help find her killer, cupid struck Eve and Kyle at first sight.

"Have fun mansion shopping," I called, waving her off. "Hey," I added before she closed the shop door and headed for her Mini Cooper parked right outside. "Have Kyle enter the Lamborghini in Brandy's vintage car show Saturday, as part of the Carousel of Love fundraiser. The Nurture Kids Foundation is his mother's kind of charity."

"Great idea. See you around." Eve closed her door but powered down her window. "Please don't tell Nick about kissing Werner until I get back, 'kay? I don't wanna miss the fun."

I gave her a dubious look. "Payback's a stitch." I watched her pout as she drove away.

My Out to Lunch sign and the click of the shop lock

became an imperative to release my breath. I needed, at the very least, a thimbleful of control and a bit of downtime to sort some sticky issues, Nick being only one of several.

I'd barely sat when the shop phone rang. "Vintage Magic; how can I dress you?"

"Give me Isobel," demanded a chipmunk with attitude before he/she/it demonstrated, not quite beneath its breath, an impressive and varied case of potty mouth. The obscenities ended with the same demand they'd started with: "Give me Isobel," delivered like Darth Vader on helium, or a squirrel on steroids; take your pick.

Isobel *York*? I wondered. The intern I was taking under my Vintage Magic wing, despite my strong—and growing stronger—reservations?

As if sensing my angst, Dante Underhill, my shop-bound ghost, appeared beside me. We couldn't even touch, my friend the resident spirit and I, but I felt safer with him beside me.

The voice, no matter how silly, carried a threat I didn't know how to answer. "I beg your pardon? Can you repeat that?" I stalled while my heart raced.

"What time is Isobel due?" the now rabid rodent asked. While less threatening than a full-out black-hearted villain, the critter hadn't yet mastered its audio modulation device.

Panicked humor aside, I gave in to a whole-body shiver. "Who is this?" I asked.

"Her *brother*," came a deeper, more cavernous voice, followed by a charged pause. "Ya hear me?" Deep Throat asked. "I'm her brother!"

So . . . I was hiring an intern I didn't want, whose *brother* best aped James Earl Jones and tiny striped rodents. Fact is, his emphasis on the word "brother" made me wonder if it might not be a woman. Voice changers could easily be set to mask gender. They were computers, after all, so Eve studied them in grad school when we lived together in New York. They could make inexperienced users sound like deep-voiced, slow-talking drones or fast-talking chipmunks. This caller was all over the map.

Dante placed his hand on his heart, like he'd protect me, and he meant it, but unless Wrath Vader stepped foot in my shop—which I so did not want—I was on my own.

Well. Not entirely on my own. I could call Detective Werner.

Yeah, that Werner. The one I *slept* with.

Not.

Two

I placed the phone on its charger and rubbed my arms. Isobel York hadn't started interning yet, and one of her theoretical relatives—who did not sound the least loving—had already scared the wooly knobby knits out of me.

Brandy, Brandy, Brandy. What do you know about this friend of a friend from the Peace Corps?

Typical Brandy. Don't get me wrong. I've missed my sister in a lot of ways. And her self-absorption came with a generous work ethic toward helping the children of the world.

But get her in range of home, and she became the six-year-old who lost her mother, expecting the world to revolve around her . . . and her causes. In the process of returning for Sherry's baby shower, she hadn't just talked me into taking on an intern; she'd imposed on me to do the prep work for several of her fund-raisers.

Not only did I agree to mentor a stranger in my shop, my father agreed to house the new intern, two promises that frightening phone call made me regret.

True, Isobel is practically paying me to take her on. She's giving me a huge trunk of her grandmother's vintage clothing, which I might or might not accept, depending on Isobel's attachment to them. That I won't know until she arrives.

The trunk itself already complemented my art deco sitting area, teasing me with its hidden treasure, especially with the key in an old manila-type pay envelope tied to the lock with a yellow ribbon.

Looking retro but well-kept, covered in pale blue antiqued alligator, it was banded with copper strips on both sides, each topped with a molded lion head.

I wanted to look inside in the worst way, but I swore it would remain closed until Isobel arrived.

I hadn't wanted an intern, but I couldn't wait for Isobel to open the trunk. Me, I can't afford to get any inadvertent psychometric vibes from the vintage clothes inside—little trick I picked up, against my will, from my mother the witch. Story for another day.

Neither do I want to become embroiled in Isobel York's family secrets, which often happens with my spontaneous and unexpected visions, though that phone call had shoved me into a parallel rock and a hard place.

Yes, *some* vintage clothes sort of "speak" to me and take me to places they've been, albeit in my mind, where I see snippets of the past, a scary kind of day tripping, I can tell you.

To be fair, I haven't read a piece of vintage clothing in months. So, perhaps—hopefully—if it pleased whatever deity controlled these things—possibly Buddha, and Yoda, too—my psychometric phase had passed.

An unexpected whiff of chocolate hit me, a sign my mother's spirit hovered, along with a clear vision of her laughing, and I sighed. Not a phase, then.

In self-defense, I turned my attention from that tempting trunk to the problem at hand.

Well, problems, plural: my intern for one, my psychic gift for another, and the ethical need to tell Nick, my FBI boy toy, about a kiss I shared with Werner, though, sewing circle oath, Werner and I *were* in a sleep-induced, half-unconscious state at the time.

My only other problem would be, you guessed it: Brandy, my bohemian sister. She who set me up as neatly as if she tied me, wrists and ankles, with a fat polka-dot bow, turquoise, maybe, with big magenta dots. Gaudy and tasteless, just to rub my face in it. I could see the funky bow in my mind's eye as if Brandy used it like a glove to slap my face.

But I never could resist a challenge, baste it.

Chakra, my butterscotch striped kitty, who, since the first time I picked her up, calmed me at my jittery solar plexus, vaulted onto my lap to cuddle, so, beat by beat, my angst receded.

"Thanks, sweetie." I stroked her behind her ears, her purr like a lullaby. "I needed that." With her in my arms, I tried to put my concerns into perspective.

I should anticipate the adventure ahead of me with Brandy's special events rather than dread her effect on my daily routine. After all, she hadn't caused chaos or panic in ages. How could she, halfway across the world?

My cell phone vibrated, revealing Brandy as my caller. I answered, since she was due home at some point tonight, and I needed to pick her up at the train station.

"Mad," she said. "Isobel and I aren't coming in on the same train after all. Some goofy bass-toned bureaucrat called my apartment and sent me on a wild-goose chase to sign missing Peace Corps termination papers, and on my way, I got mugged. My bag got torn right off me. My neck's killing me."

"Oh, no. Are you all right?"

"Couple aspirin, some muscle cream, and I'll be fine. But it was all for nothing. My termination papers weren't missing."

I so hoped the bass-toned bureaucrat wasn't Isobel's very own Wrath Vader. "What are you going to do without your purse?"

"Backpack. Cops found it in a trash can a couple blocks down, everything inside but my train ticket. Doesn't matter. I had already missed the train. Isobel will have boarded in D.C., expecting to connect with me when I boarded here in New York, so she'll be there before me, like maybe five minutes ago? Be a dear and pick her up at the station, will you? Look for me around six thirtyish?"

"Pick up Isobel now? Bran, this is the middle of my workday. You didn't even ballpark me on the time."

"Didn't I? Hmm." She hung up, just like that, assuming I'd take care of everything.

Justified, I acknowledged without guilt the validity of my angst. How could I have forgotten for a deluded moment the way Brandy—bossy and with a smile—tended to spark chaos among the family, making the most flexible of us smolder and sometimes burn?

I was betting that Professor Harry Cutler, my eventempered father, would be the first to blow.

Three

I base my fashion sense on what doesn't itch.
—GILDA RADNER

I clapped my phone shut.

Okay, so the mix-up wasn't my sister's fault, but she *could* have called at the time she *missed* the train, rather than six and a half hours later, five minutes *after* I was supposed to meet it.

Suppose I had . . . customers . . . a doctor's appointment . . . my car in the shop?

Ticking off beneath my breath a lifetime of similar incidents, I crated Chakra for the few minutes I'd be gone, locked the shop, and backed my Honda Element from the lot.

I'd had it painted lavender to match my building, with a small replica of my sign painted on its side: Vintage Magic in bold white on an eggplant shield. Behind the

13

name stood a pale lavender side silhouette of a woman who could be Jackie O.

It was like my calling card, and people waved whenever they saw it.

I waited to turn left, from Bank Street to Main, noting the brisk business at Mystic Pizza, fast-moving as always, *unlike* the snail-crawling traffic on Main.

While I waited, I tried not to judge my world-traveling middle sister for her foibles, though being me, I couldn't help but wince at her wardrobe choices. Brandy subscribes to the Gilda Radner school of fashion, which many would call smart.

I am not one of them.

Brandy is comfortable in her skin and needs no outer trappings to feel good about herself. I envy that, to a point. Me, I'm still willing to itch a little for a smart look or the right guy. Well, make that two right guys. I groaned and touched my forehead. That sure makes me the stable one.

As for Brandy's personality, well . . . in the same way that I, Madeira Cutler, am my mother's daughter, psychic abilities and all, my sister Brandy—third Cutler, but second daughter—resembles . . . no one, really.

While Brandy denies the existence of the metaphysical gifts mom left me and scoffs at my love of vintage fashion, she's not beyond soliciting my wealthy clients to seed her newest and most worthy cause, which will require a lot of work in the next few days . . . on *my* part.

They are worthy, Brandy's causes; I mean that. But they are also many and oft-changing.

Where my father, the English professor, quotes literary greats, Brandy quotes philanthropists and world hunger organizations. I admire her for her generosity, thoughtfulness, and fortitude and for giving up her eternal stint in the Peace Corps to raise money for a good cause.

To be fair, she planned her fund-raising trip to coincide with our sister Sherry's baby shower next Sunday. Well, Brandy did delay the event a little with her schedule, but we're still safe having it in June, because the baby isn't due until July.

Sherry's father-in-law, Justin Vancortland IV, aka Cort, is lending Brandy his property—gatehouse, manse, lawns, and gardens—for Saturday's fund-raiser. The day will feature a ride on Scotland's famous MacKenzie Carousel on world tour and a fifties car show with models dressed in the style of the decade. It'll culminate that evening with a fifties dress ball and bachelor auction. An altogether fun event, if I can get past planning it.

Brandy and Cort shared barbs at Sherry's wedding. She ribbed him for his wealth. Cort, to give him credit, gave as good as he got. They made fine sparring partners, not to mention dancing and dinner partners, as well. The thing is: *I* dressed Brandy for Sherry's wedding. Nuff said.

Cort seemed to appreciate Brandy's zeal for solving

world hunger, so much so that he gave her a hefty donation. Better than good cooking as a way to Brandy's heart. Sure, nearly two decades separated them. But Brandy was an old soul, if ever I'd met one, and the Peace Corps had a way of maturing people beyond their years. Secretly, I thought they complemented each other, but hey, playing cupid wasn't my forte.

Bottom line, they'd connected on several levels, deeper than a donation could accomplish. But to pick up where they left off might entail an itchy outfit or three and shoes that didn't flip when Brandy flopped.

Still stuck on Bank Street with my car idling, I was steaming for so many reasons. With my luck, some three-masted schooner was waiting for the Department of Transportation to raise the Mystic River Drawbridge so it could sail into the Fishers Island Sound beyond the harbor—a sight I found spectacular on a good day, which would not be today by any stretch of the imagination, mystic, psychic, or spastic.

Yes, in case you haven't guessed, the Mystic River Drawbridge sits square between me and the Mystic Train Station.

Stopping for a slow-moving sailboat would put me at the train station at, oh, twenty-five minutes past rude. Not a good way to meet your new intern, with both of you steaming.

Isobel York, according to Brandy, had applied for a fashion design reality show more than once and never *quite* made it. She'd attended fashion school between modeling jobs and was supposed to be a talented designer.

So why be *my* intern?

"She wants to learn at the hands of a master." That's the scrap Brandy handed me, anyway. Yeah, barf.

Isobel, an independent, sought-after fashion model, works regularly for a top modeling agency, and she conned her wealthy boss, Madame Celine Robear, into attending Brandy's fund-raiser.

Sure, Robear has an iffy rep, but having the modeling mogul in attendance will be a coup for Brandy in her new role as development director for the Nurture Kids Foundation. And I get to utilize the models Madame Celine is bringing for the fifties car show and as usherettes for the bachelor auction.

Traffic opened; I nudged my way onto Main, and luck stayed with me. The drawbridge remained down, and the seagulls skirting the grave in traffic, while scrabbling over spilled fries, would live to be roadkill another day.

Despite expectations to the contrary, I reached my destination two and a half minutes early, though the train—always late—beat me.

This must be a cold day in hell.

Mystic's train station projected a quaint landmark beauty. Small and painted cream, its Victorian architectural trim a rusty orange, it was used as a model for a toy train terminal by American Flyer in the fifties.

I parked in the lot, waited, and remembered that only passengers on the southbound trains exited station side. Meanwhile, the northbound motored to life and disappeared around the bend, revealing a swarm of motion across the tracks. A humming throng faced into the open-front, three-sided platform shelter where commuters waited in bad weather.

While one or two focused arrivals—places to go, things to do—cut across the tracks bisecting Broadway Avenue, they first had to skirt an ambulance, shelter side, its spinning bubble light speeding my heart.

My sudden panic became rooted in strange phone calls, and I sprinted along Broadway to the opposite side of the tracks, re-creating a scene from *Up the Down Staircase* as I flowed against the disembarking crowd. An unconscious girl lay on the bench in the commuter shelter, paramedics checking her vitals.

An unexpected shiver of unease scuttled through me.

Presiding over the scene: Detective Lytton Werner, or "Little Wiener" as I'd dubbed him in third grade. Call ours a grudging relationship, except when awareness sizzled, as it unfortunately did one "thermonuclear night"—his words.

He gave me a double take. "Madeira, don't tell me you know this girl?"

"Never saw her before. But I won't kid you; for a half a sec, I feared it was Brandy." Relief flooded my senses. "I'm here to pick up my new intern. Name's Isobel.

Anybody ask directions?" I glanced back across the tracks toward the terminal, shading my eyes from the sun.

"Isobel?" Werner asked. "Isobel who?"

"Isobel York," I said.

At the instant set of his lips, I nearly tripped over my own feet. He led me away from the crowd.

"What?" I asked, stopping, unable to wrap my mind around his sudden handle-with-care attitude.

"Mad," Lytton said. Jaw set, he looked over at the medics, and moved his hand from my arm to the flat of my back to turn me and block my peripheral vision, the warmth of his hand, his ploy and nearness rushing pin-pricks to my limbs.

"We checked her ID, Mad. That's Isobel York on the bench. She didn't make it."

Four

Women are now more comfortable with themselves and their bodies—they no longer feel the need to hide behind their clothes.
— DONNA KARAN

"No," I said, reeling. "My Isobel York"—the intern I *hadn't* wanted in the first place—"can't be dead. She's coming to work with me. She's young and vibrant and alive."

"You're in denial," Werner said. "That's normal. It's okay."

"Don't patronize me!" I jerked my hand from his grasp so hard, he looked appalled, like I'd turned on him, while he rubbed his wrist as if he'd twisted it or I had.

He took a count-to-ten breath, as if he needed patience . . . or a weapon. "Madeira, I understand that you're upset," he said, "but—"

I glanced back at the poor soul on the bench. "You know what? That girl *can't* be my intern."

I could almost see steam rising from his collar. "Okay, Madeira, I'll bite. Why can't she be your intern?"

"Isobel York is a fashionista, a glamazon. But this girl is wearing yoga pants, a peasant blouse, and ankle socks with jelly sandals. And her purse; well, I can only describe that as an electric blue plastic Prodo."

"What's a Prodo?"

"Neither a Prada *nor* a fashion statement."

Werner shrugged. "Her socks are peach like her peasant blouse."

As if that made her fashionable.

"Yeah, red shoes and peach socks." I brushed the hair from my eyes. "I rest my case."

"Maybe she's poor."

"Poor, not blind. But she isn't . . . poor, I mean. I'm guessing a fashion plate walked out of this crowd without her wallet, though she doesn't know it yet."

Werner looked around. "I don't see a fashion plate waiting for a ride, Mad." He gave his assistant a nod with a double gimme palm-up curl of his fingers.

Billings handed him a Coach Wallet. Werner opened it and showed me the dead girl's driver's license. Isobel York, it said, and her picture, well . . . I stepped closer to the body—I mean, the girl—to compare it to her face, trying not to focus on those hard-set blue lips or the purpling beneath her eyes and unpolished fingernails.

"They're . . . identical." A feeling of abject helplessness rose in me. I turned from the sight, and when Werner put an arm around my waist to walk me away from the crowd once more, I took full advantage of his support, not sure I could have made it on my own.

"Sorry to be such a pain, Detective. I feel . . . responsible. Entirely so. Like she . . . died on my watch." True, I'd never met her and she'd died before reaching me, but still, I'd hired her, and now she was dead. "Lytton, what happened to her?"

"You mean, how did she die?" Werner asked. "That's not readily apparent. You know that pinpointing cause of death can be a maze of thorns, with a—you'll excuse the pun—dead end or two along the way."

I stepped back. "Is that how you see your job?"

He gave me a look filled with meaning. "Only when I work with you."

Whoa, I thought, trying to pull my gaze from his. Did that make me exciting? Or a pain in the butt seam?

His steely regard reminded me that his hands and mouth knew me better than he did.

I shivered and hated myself for it.

"Well," he said, "I guess my job isn't all thorns and free falls. Sometimes there's thermonuclear activity."

I could deny it till doomsday, and yet the magic of his signature scent, Armani Black Code, mixed with his particular male musk revved my libido even now. "You can retire your Geiger counter, Detective." Liar, liar, don't preach to the choir.

"We'll see," he said with an eye twinkle that disappeared fast, his attention suddenly on his notebook. "Any idea where Ms. York boarded the train?"

"Washington, D.C., I believe."

"Time of death will tell us if she made it to this spot from the train on her own or if someone carried her here." He eyed me for a minute. "It'll also tell us *where* she died. She could have been killed in Baltimore, Philadelphia, New York, or New Jersey, which would mean that her body was transported across state lines. You know what that means. Puts a whole new perspective on the investigation."

"Great, this could turn into a federal investigation."

"We *would* have to work with the Feds."

Scrap silk and little bone buttons! I did *not* want Werner and Nick working anywhere *near* each other.

"How's Nick these days?" Werner asked, too interested.

"On assignment, as if you care."

Werner knew I hadn't come clean with my on-again, off-again FBI hunk and a half about the thermonuclear kiss Werner and I shared, a rather large elephant standing between us right now.

Bless him, though, he passed on mentioning the screaming pachyderm and cleared his throat. "I can't believe you're involved in another suspicious death, Miss Cutler."

Miss Cutler all of a sudden? Ah, I got it. The gentleman side of the formidable detective had not only given it a pass, but he put a safe, comfortable distance between us and it.

I hoped that I could keep from thanking him and focusing attention where I wanted it least, on us. I also prayed my guilt remained invisible, because God knew, though we'd been half-asleep at the time, that had been one hell of a kiss we were ignoring.

I couldn't show my gratitude, but I tipped my metaphorical hat by turning him back into my nemesis, where he belonged, and giving him what he expected from me, *attitude*. "How do you know Isobel didn't die of natural causes? Jumping the gun, aren't we?"

"Are we?" he asked. "Were we? Or do we want more of the same?"

Yowsa! And I thought we'd reverted to dealing with one another on a professional basis. My mistake. Where's an oven mitt when you need one?

It just went to show that in a town this size, you couldn't avoid each other forever, but I'd had a pretty good run.

At the moment, however, I ignored him by shaking my hair from my face to collect my wits. "The case, Detective." I reminded us both. "The girl in the platform shelter?"

"Sorry, some things just stay with a man. The girl. Natural causes. Good point. We don't know, yet. Forensics will have something to say about that, I'm sure."

"I thought so." I went for snooty, a side of me he

knew best from our school days and liked least. "I don't even know the girl," I said, disliking the mournful hitch in my chest. "She's Brandy's friend. I didn't even *want* to hire her."

I grabbed his wrist. "Lytton, you don't think Brandy could be in danger? They were supposed to be on the same train, but my sister called to say she'd be in later."

"That you talked to Brandy is a good sign. I'd think she was safer *not* traveling with Ms. York this trip." He tilted his head. "If you talked to her, why did you think it could be her?"

"Panic knows no logic. So, Isobel's death really *could* have been an accident?" I bit my lip.

"There are usually visible signs with an accidental death, while malicious intent often has to be ferreted out."

"I hate it when you're right." Feeling emotionally battered and bruised, I turned to leave.

"Madeira?" Werner called.

I stopped and looked back, hope rising in me.

"Stay close. No out-of-town buying trips for the next few days."

"Why? I'm not even a witness."

"Right. You're the deceased's reluctant employer."

"Tucking A!" I turned on my heel and speed-dialed Brandy while I took a wide berth around the ambulance and crossed Broadway, before the railroad crossing barriers came down. While I stood hyperventilating in the

25

depot parking lot, more frantic at each unanswered ring, Brandy picked up on the seventh.

That's when my heart started beating again.

"Mad, can't talk now. I'm about to board the train."

"Call me when you get in," I said. "And, Sis, be careful."

"On a train? Silly Mad. Your inner sleuth is eating your brain."

"Yeah, *that's* my problem." I watched the sheeted gurney disappear into the ambulance, clapped my phone shut, turned toward my car, and released the sob I'd been fighting to hold back.

Five

Life must go on, which seemed wrong, I thought, with less bounce in my step as I got back into my utility vehicle, mired in a whole lot of guilt for not wanting Isobel York in my life. Worse, if I hadn't given in to Brandy's nagging and had said a firm *"no"* to taking on her friend, Isobel might still be alive. If it was an accident.

Premeditated, it would have happened anyway, anywhere.

At the shop, life snapped me back to normal, whether I wanted it to or not, when I found the Sweets, Ethel the younger, in her eighties, Dolly's daughter-in-law, and Dolly herself, the town centenarian and my ghost Dante Underhill's old flame.

Dolly could also see Dante, which is why she "shopped" here often.

But today a third woman, a stranger to Mystic, wearing a pricey Vivienne Westwood suit, waited with them. She was about Ethel's age, and though Ethel admitted they'd never met, they'd struck up a friendly conversation. Odd, because Ethel didn't do friendly well.

Bette gave no last name, almost on purpose, but her calling card sat in the parking lot, a powder blue stretch limo, chauffeur included.

Like Brandy said, sleuthing could be eating my brain, because I made a pretense of going back to my car so I could glance at the limo's plate. Rhode Island. Y-1. Call me nuts, but in New England that's like confessing to sleeping with a senator or congressman. Or to investing heavily in a campaign. Same thing.

Pushing Isobel and sleuthing to the back of my mind, I turned to concentrating on my job. Customers come first and all that. The three clicked as they checked out the fashions of their day and reminisced, though Ethel and Bette barely noticed when Dolly and Dante got lost in Shoe Heaven.

I made tea and set out the cookies Dolly brought me. Let's face it, women who buy vintage at high-end designer specialty shops had a lot of the little girl left in them. They still loved playing dress-up, being pampered, and having tea parties, which pretty much summed up my line of work. Except I could indulge my shopaholic tendencies whenever I wanted, with Vintage Magic as my excuse.

My other love, designing clothes, I also made part and parcel of my work. Did I have a dream job or what?

Over tea, the ladies tended to talk fast and at the same time, though they never failed to surprise me by managing a true exchange of information. As for me, I rarely got a word in, edgewise or otherwise, and they never noticed unless they wanted my opinion.

The only spooky moment of their visit happened when Bette stood looking down at Isobel's trunk for an uncomfortably long time.

"Do you have an assistant, Miss Cutler?" she asked.

Like a knife came the memory of Isobel on that bench. "No, no, I don't."

"But you will soon," Dolly said. The Sweets practically raised my siblings after my mother passed, and I kept them in the loop.

"Everything's a bit up in the air intern-wise at the moment," I said, and Bette firmed her lips.

After the ladies left, that trunk whispered my name louder than ever. Why had a stranger stared so long at it? Why ask such a pointed, spot-on question? Maybe she was a bit psychic, too. I'd never know. She said she was only passing through. I made a note to ask Eve to do a little digging on the number of the plate.

I did wonder after that if the trunk might hold a clue as to what happened to Isobel, but I resisted opening it.

I'd ask Werner if he found a relative to identify the body, because I had something of Isobel's to give them. Fact was, maybe I had evidence.

As a distraction, I forced myself to work on the book-keeping system Eve programmed for me, so I wouldn't rush over and tear open the key envelope with my teeth.

A magic word—"key"—in relationship to a suspicious death. Sadly, that was one yellow ribbon not meant to welcome Isobel York.

My thoughts turned on a dime. A yellow ribbon. I didn't have an oak tree, but I whipped up a fat yellow bow, went out, and tied it to my Element's passenger side rearview mirror to welcome Brandy home in a positive way. Too bad I'd have to greet her with bad news.

The shop phone rang, so I went back inside.

Reminded of my creepazoid morning caller, I answered with trepidation, only now putting the anomalous caller and my dead intern in the same range of possibility. "Vintage Magic, how can I dress you?"

"Is she there yet?" Likely one and the same voice. Wrath Vader had possibly mastered his modulator, now evoking a deep evil or an alien from outer space.

"Is who here?"

"Isobel. Let me talk to Izzy." Did the vocal inflection change with her name, a hint of satisfaction, like the creepamagog might have grinned, knowing he asked for the impossible. Werner would need to know who, among her acquaintants, called Isobel "Izzy."

"I just sent her on an errand for me," I lied. You can't get no . . . sa-tis-fac-shun. "I'll be glad to tell her you called. Is this her brother again? May I have your number?"

He called me ugly names and with two succinct words, not "tuck you," the sleaze hung up.

My hands shook again as I picked up my cell phone and hit speed dial.

As Werner answered, Nick walked in. But I'd lost my ability to speak.

Italian stallion in the flesh. Five o'clock shadow. Deep, dark, bedroom eyes eating me up with his gaze. A half nod and an attempt not to show me how hungry he was for the sight of me.

I knew because I attempted the same.

Werner called my name over the phone loud enough for Nick to hear and comment. "You'd better talk to him before he busts a blood vessel."

"Werner," I said. "Sorry. I've had a scare."

Nick looked sharply up at me and scanned the room.

I told Werner about the ugly drone calls, glad Nick could hear me. I also outlined Brandy's delaying call: her mugging and lost train ticket. "Do you think they could be related to Isobel's death?" I asked.

Nick's spine went rigid, and he stood close enough to tease me with the musky ambergris scent in his Ultraviolet Man cologne.

"Nothing is related if the girl died of natural causes," Werner said. "We got a positive ID, by the way."

"What do you mean, you got a positive? Who identified her?"

"Madame Celine Robear. Ms. York had the woman's business card behind her license."

"I know the name. She owns the modeling agency where Isobel works. She's coming to Mystick Falls next weekend for Brandy's fund-raiser."

"I know. I called the number on the card and—you're not going to believe this—the woman was on a train from Boston, half an hour out. I met her, she got off, came to the morgue, identified the body as that of Isobel York, and she caught the next train back to the Big Apple."

"That was too easy," I said. "Too much of a coincidence."

Nick gave me a thumbs-up.

"How upset did she seem?" I asked Werner.

"Very upset."

"Too upset?"

"Look, Mad, some IDs are easy," Werner assured me, "but most aren't."

Nick shrugged his reluctant agreement to that.

I rolled my eyes. "Describe Robear to me in, say, two words."

"Voluptuous."

"I don't mean her body, I mean her demeanor, and that's only one word, you sex maniac."

Nick raised both brows. Guess I shouldn't have divulged my knowledge of that truism.

"Self-assured," Werner said, continuing to describe her, unaware of the undercurrents. "Comfortable in her skin. Educated. Sophisticated. Celine Robear seamlessly aces a perfect balance in the feminine mystique-to-businesswoman ratio."

"And I don't?"

Nick wagged a finger at me.

I frowned.

Werner coughed. "You asked me to describe the owner of Flair Robear. I'd have a whole different description of you."

One I did not want to hear with my sexy ex standing beside me and racing my heart. "So, you're saying Celine Robear didn't look like a killer?"

"Who does? But don't worry, I ordered a background check."

"Good. I mean, suppose Isobel didn't die of natural causes and her killer stayed on the train to the end of the line, turned around for the return trip, and you caught her halfway back?"

"I checked Robear's alibi. Plus her hotel vouches for her. That would be one weekend keynote speaker for the Regal Grace, Supermodels of Tomorrow Conference, present and accounted for. I plan to get hotel videotapes of the entire event. Robear was taking interviews for her agency and speaking."

My heart tripped. "Isobel York really did die?" I whispered. I hadn't wanted to believe it.

"'Fraid so, Mad," Werner said. "Besides, she looked just like the picture on her license. As for those digitized calls, I'll get a wiretap on your phone as soon as possible. Tomorrow at the latest. I'm sorry about your intern, kiddo."

I wiped my eyes with the back of a hand. "Thanks, Lytton." I hung up.

Nick took me in his arms to comfort me, and being there felt like coming home. I had a good cry. Probably not just for Isobel. I'd missed Nick more than I dared admit. "Is my brother okay? Did he come home, too?"

"Your brother, Alex, my ace FBI partner, is especially okay now that he's home with his wife and daughter. He's got a week off, so I'm on my own for now. His little Kelsey is just like you."

"How is she like me?" I asked, not quite done with my cry, because even that notion brought tears to my eyes.

"For one thing she toddled into my room at dawn, and before I woke up, she gave me a drink of water. Yeah, I was flat on my back asleep, and she held my nightstand glass of water to my lips."

My bubble of laughter turned to tears, because I missed this about us. This sharing the little things.

"Let it out, ladybug. Sounds like you've been having a bad time."

I smacked him in the chest with the flat of a hand. "Because you left, you big lug. Staying away so long, changing your cell phone number. Today I got threatening calls, then my intern got murdered, or she died of natural causes at the ripe old age of twenty-something, and could I call you? No! I mean, my sister-in-law told me it was going to be a while, but, well, you didn't."

He rested his chin on my head. "I'm back, ladybug. And I'm sorry."

"For how long?"

"I'll be sorry forever, but I'm back for as long my new case lasts. Unless you want me to leave?"

"What case?" I stepped from his arms and ignored the question, because right now, yeah, I wanted him here. "Your case is not *my* case?"

"Of course not. You're not in law enforcement. The case belongs to me and your brother when he gets back to work, and it's not about Isobel's death. How could I get home so fast for something that happened this morning? However, it might be related. I need to talk to Werner about that. And if you tell your brother you know even that much, I'll deny it. If my case impacts yours, I'll bring you into the loop, okay?"

"Okay."

"Now, you got something thermonuclear you wanna tell me about?"

Six

Fashion is only the attempt to realize art in living forms and
social intercourse.   —FRANCIS BACON

"Who have you been talking to?" I snapped.

Nick's chin dimple deepened with his chuckle. "Eve.
She just saw me walking back to my car for my cell
phone, and she assumed you'd confessed, and I was
leaving. So she gloated, of course, and let her X-rated
version of the cat out of the bag."

"I'm gonna kill her." I tried to charge out the door to
annihilate my BFF, but Nick held me back with an arm
across my bodice and a grasp on my far shoulder, his
chesty chuckle soothing my senses.

I liked it, drat my traitorous body. The feel, scent, and
sound of him. Having him near.

"Eve's gone," he said. "Kyle dragged her back to his
car with his hand over her mouth, strapped her into the

Lamborghini, and drove away. Mad, she's such a good friend to you, and her dislike of me is so deliciously amusing. I hardly have to work to keep her ticked. Besides, I welcomed her enhanced truth. It was tame compared to the worst-case scenarios I started conjuring when not otherwise occupied in the trenches."

That caught my attention; the trenches meant danger, and all this time, he'd been as upset as me. Right now, I couldn't address either.

He'd hurt me. Judged me and found me guilty without hearing my side, so I got stubborn and didn't tell him anything. Not about Tasering Werner so I had to drag him to my bed or about passing out there myself because I got a psychometric reading. Sure, half-asleep, we shared a kiss. So what. But I let Nick think the worst and broke up with him.

"Give me your new cell phone number," I said, rather pouty, so he'd try to charm me out of it.

He picked up my phone and programmed his new number into it. "Am I still number one?"

"Speed dial wise? Yes."

He grinned and set the phone back down on my counter. "Now, tell me," he said, hands on my shoulders, so comfortably and comfortingly close, "why you agreed to an intern and what happened to her."

Peace settled into my bones as I told Nick about Brandy, every detail about the train station and the phone calls. "I know I complained at first about having an intern," I admitted, "but I'm honestly sorry I'm not going to get to work with Isobel. I had begun to believe I could help her."

Nick raised a brow. "She's not beyond help. No one ever is. Find her some justice. Was she in trouble? Running away? On drugs? You have your own ways to get answers. Get sleuthing."

"Oh, no," I said, shaking my head while putting away discarded outfits. "I will not get mixed up in another murder investigation."

"Sounds like you already are. Didn't you just call it your case?"

I shrugged. Drat him for calling me on it. "My case as in Isobel was my intern, and that's all, until now."

"The caller who threatened Isobel before she died," Nick said, "has your number. That scares me. Get proactive. I missed you. Take care of yourself. I don't want to make missing you a permanent situation."

He pulled me to him as if he couldn't help himself.

That hit me square in the heart; then he gave me a look that turned my knees to jelly, but I tried to remain strong.

When I succeeded, he raised both hands from my shoulders and stepped back, as if trying not to touch me, and he leaned against the sitting area wall and crossed his arms and ankles. "You have genuine talent. Shame to waste it. You can always bounce your psychometric visions off me. Eve sure doesn't want to hear about your readings."

"I also have a talent that requires designing and wallowing in vintage fashion."

"I have a need to spend time with you. Unofficially, FBI-wise. Off-again, boy-toy-wise."

"You could have come back sooner."

He straightened. "No, according to the rules of undercover FBI work, I couldn't. Let's say . . . I was forced to stay beneath a certain level on the whereabouts radar screen; that's why my phone got canceled."

He stepped closer and crossed my lips with a finger. "Now, in addition to your design ability, you read vintage clothes with tales to tell."

Only a few people knew about my ability, including him and Eve, when it came to reading vintage clothes. "Yes, but that's like a universal mandate, and there's no way—" I caught my breath and looked over at Isobel's trunk. Wooly knobby knits, the darned thing was practically calling my name. Talk about a universal imperative.

"You've already begun to sense that trouble is brewing, haven't you, ladybug? It only works if you listen, you know." He caught the direction of my gaze. "Take that trunk—"

"No. You take it." And though I didn't want to, I made my way to the alligator trunk in the corner of the room. "This, I fear, is a problem of the psychometric variety."

"It reeks of secrets," Nick said. "I'll give you that, and it looks to have belonged to a kindred spirit of yours, someone who dresses like a million bucks."

I sighed, remorse overtaking me again in a day full of regrets.

"Where did you get it, and what's supposed to be inside?" Nick asked.

"You were right in guessing it has relevance to Isobel's murder. It's full of vintage clothes. Isobel York's grandmother's. Isobel wanted me to have them in exchange for teaching her my design techniques, but I'm not sure I should keep them now."

"If you want to turn your back on your gift, send it back."

I checked the return address on the label and sat hard on my fainting couch. "I can't. Isobel put my father's address as her return address. She was going to stay with us while she worked here."

Nick raised a brow. "I guess the trunk and all that's in it are yours to do with what you . . . must?"

"If I opened it, I'd feel like I was invading somebody's privacy. And if the clothes inside do hold secrets, do I have the right to them?"

"Only if knowing will help find Isobel's killer. I know I doubted your ability to read clothes at first, but now I respect the hell out of it."

I laid my head on his shoulder. "I haven't read any vintage clothes since February, so I was thinking I might be done with that."

"But the unexplained death of the girl who owned the

trunk might taunt your psychic gift. If I were the investigator, I'd welcome your help."

"I missed you, Nick, and I'm sorry I wasn't straight with you about the kiss. Your lack of trust, well, it wounded me."

He looked beaten. "I understand why you didn't tell me what happened. You were innocent, and I judged you. You have nothing to be sorry for. I do. And I apologize for taking a job I knew would last for months without telling you. I'm as guilty of avoiding the issue as you are, and without your good reasons. Let's go back to being friends, and see what happens? Wha'd'ya say?"

No matter what he said, I believed he wanted things to go back the way they'd been between us since I returned to Mystick Falls, and I hated to give him false hope. When I lived in New York, he rarely visited, though we talked on the phone often. Friends—we had been friends then.

When I moved home, we picked up where we left off without thinking much about it—spontaneous combustion and all—but Nick still took me as much for granted as he did when I lived in the Big Apple. And I just wasn't sure I could handle our semi-committed relationship. It felt like limbo: Would we ever move forward into something more serious? Did I want to? Did he? Maybe I needed a break from the hot and sexy part of our "friendship" to sort it all out.

"I have to go pick up Brandy, and since I need reinforcements, my dad's waiting for me to pick him up."

Nick got up as if to let me do my thing, hands in his tight black jeans pockets, like he didn't know quite where to put himself.

I opened my arms, and he walked into them for an embrace and a too-friendly kiss. So I stepped back. "I accept your offer. We were friends when I lived in New York. I think we could be again. I've missed you, Nick. I've missed my friend. I want to call you anytime and talk things over with you, except for when you're working, of course."

He released a breath, and his shoulders relaxed. "I'd like that. You look spectacular," he said.

"It means a lot that *you* think so. You look pretty great, too. You should know that Werner and I are becoming friends. I had dinner with him a couple of times while you were gone."

"I understand," Nick said. "May the best friend win?"

"This isn't a competition."

"The hell it isn't," he muttered.

I smoothed his furrowed brow, kissed his cheek, and urged him out the door. Friends. They were both just friends, I reminded myself.

I felt better about Nick and me as he drove off.

I grabbed my vintage Ralph Lauren purse with RLL woven into the fabric, engraved on the strap hook and upholstery tacks. Ralph's initials hung from one of its three gold fobs, the other two being a stirrup and a horse head. These days, you were lucky if you got one fob on a Ralph Lauren purse.

Just an old black purse, Brandy might say . . . with Ralph's signature all over it. I grinned despite myself, feeling better about Nick than I had in months.

He might be right about the trunk. I'd think about opening it later.

I saw him still idling at the corner in his noisy diesel-fueled Hummer, and watched until he disappeared onto Main Street.

After I got in the car, I noticed that my shop door hadn't bounced shut. It would have locked when it did, but it remained open. So I got out of the car and went to see why.

Dante stood just inside the shop, arms crossed. "Madeira Cutler, *I* want to know about the thermonuclear kiss you shared with the Wiener. You've been holding out on me." He wagged a finger and gave me his knee-weakening smile.

I did have some good looking hunks in my life.

Dante frowned. "Promise you'll tell me."

"I'll tell you. Because, really, who are *you* going to tell?"

He lowered his hands to his sides. "Okay, then."

"Are you keeping my door open?"

"Yes. Are you proud of me? It's a new skill, thanks to you. I've been tapping into all the energy in here. This place is really hopping these days, and I love it. Did you know that *your* powers are spiking?"

"What powers?"

"Tell me about the thermonuclear kiss; I'll tell you about your powers." The door shut and locked between us.

I wanted to go back in and make Dante tell me everything he knew now, but I needed to fetch my dear *sweet* sister.

I looked at my watch. Ack! "Dante Underhill, I'll get you for this," I called.

A minute later, as I backed out of my parking lot, I saw Dante in an upstairs window tilting his top hat forward and giving me a cheeky grin.

Seven

Design is not an ambush . . . it's a relationship. You have to know how people move and live and work to be able to design for them.
                                    —GENEVIEVE GORDER

Ten minutes later, my dad got into my Honda while I sat with it idling in our circular drive.

"Hey, cranky man, can't you smile today?"

He grunted.

"Are you cantankerous because you haven't seen Fiona in more than a week?"

My father turned my way. "I feel a quote coming on."

"God help me," I said, and I meant it.

"Blame it on your incorrect judgment," my father said.

"I blame it on your need to punish me for my *correct* judgment."

He went for a frown and ended up chuckling. " 'A lively and lasting sense of filial duty is more effectually

45

impressed on the mind of a son or daughter by reading *King Lear*, than by all the dry volumes of ethics, and divinity, that ever were written.' Thomas Jefferson."

"Oh no, are you going to force-feed me *King Lear*? Again?"

"Don't say you don't love it when I do."

"I'm pleading the fifth." Getting my father's attention when we were children meant asking him to read a story. We didn't expect to understand his choice, but we asked and listened anyway, because the cost of his attention was priceless, and he pounced around the room acting out all the parts, which never failed to entertain us, no matter how old we got. "Loosen up," I said. "She won't be gone forever."

He barely turned my way. "Who?"

I pulled into the Mystic Train Station parking lot for the second time that day. "Dad, you're such a bad actor. I'm talking about Aunt Fiona, of course."

"She's *not* your aunt," he said. "We're *not* related."

Since Brandy's train was about five minutes out yet, we sat in the car. "Dad, about your relationship with 'skip-the-aunt' Fiona—"

"Non-relationship!" he snapped.

I raised a brow. "Yeah, that. Fee was Mom's best friend. Mom doesn't mind, Dad. She's been gone twenty years. She's cheering you on."

"Are you telling me you can see ghosts now, too?" He turned away and stared out the window.

I donned some armor, figuratively speaking, and raised my warrior's shield. "No, Dad. I don't see them, *now*. I've been seeing them since they smiled down at me in my crib."

My father whipped his gaze at me.

And since I had his full attention, I confessed. "I specifically remember telling Mom that Emma and Ronalda played tea party with me."

"Madeira? Who are Emma and Ronalda?"

"A barmaid and chambermaid, circa 1780 or so. They lived and died at our house when it was a coaching inn on the Old Boston Post Road."

"Oh, and I suppose they told you that?"

"No, the style of their clothes did."

"Fashion." He raised his hands. "Of course. And you say you told Mom about seeing them?"

"Yes and she warned me not to mention them, because nobody but us could see them. It was our secret." I grinned because I'd damned near just cracked the wall he'd erected when he found out about my mother's gifts.

"Mamma was humoring you," he said, though he didn't sound convinced himself.

"Dad, to this day, Emma and Ronalda stand in the taproom window and wave when I get home."

He opened the car door. "I won't hear or discuss this nonsense."

I got out, as well. "Fine. Listen, you've been antsy for days. If it's not Aunt Fee, is it because Brandy's coming home?"

"Of course not! Remarks like that are what make your poor sister think she's an annoying middle child." He set his lips in a firm line, the one I knew meant: Some lies must be told.

I hadn't become a successful surrogate mother to my siblings at the age of ten without learning to read my father. "Dad, Brandy is your 'get-caught-in-my-crazies' child. She has the personality of a thoughtless tornado, upsetting our calm at her whim, tossing us hither and yon, and leaving us bruised in her wake, without a 'scuse me' or an 'if you please.'"

"She would resent that, if she heard you."

"Of course she would, which doesn't mean I'm wrong." His lack of denial spoke volumes.

We made our way to the station-side platform, dad checking his watch, me eyeing the crime scene tape and investigators across the tracks combing the platform shelter and nearby for clues.

"What's with the police?" my father asked.

"You know that intern of mine who's supposed to be staying with us?"

"She'll be coming in with Brandy, right?"

"No, she won't be." My throat closed then, and I couldn't elaborate. If I had to say it, I'd only say it once, when Brandy got there.

The northbound train stopped in front of us, and Brandy would be forced to get off on the crime scene side. Still, we stayed near the homey terminal side, in the area radiating history, safety, and welcome.

When the train cleared the track, we watched its passengers crossing Broadway en masse.

"Did she get taller, decide to wear dresses, grow a Mohawk?" my father asked. "I don't see her."

"Heck," I said. "She could have blue hair, for all I know." My cell phone rang.

"Talk to me," I said, having read Brandy's name on the screen before I opened my phone.

"Sorry, Sis, I met an old friend I barely remembered from the Peace Corps, and she talked me into getting off in Philadelphia for lunch. I thought I'd catch the next train, but I missed it. Just a blip in my plans, really. I'll be in around sixish tomorrow night."

"*Tomorrow* night?"

"I'm sleeping in a bed tonight. I've had it with anything less, and sitting up in a train is way less. Look for me tomorrow, 'kay?"

Click. My phone went dead.

Look for her?

I'd look for her. With a basting gun, I'd look for her.

Eight

Fashion is at once both caterpiller and butterfly. Be a caterpiller by day and a butterfly by night.   —COCO CHANEL

In the wee hours of the following morning, I sat straight
up in my bed, my heart racing like Amtrak's Acela past
a no-stop terminal.

It took me a minute to identify the sound; not steel
wheels on steel track but a persistent and untimely intruder overworking our ancient door knocker, bound and
determined to give our iron eagle a concussion.

I put on my robe and slipped my open cell phone in
my pocket, my finger above the two, the speed dial number for Lytton's private cell phone.

When I turned on the light in the front stairs, the
knocking stopped.

Dad came out of the gentleman's parlor as I hit the
bottom of the stairs, looking like he'd never gone to bed.

I checked the grandfather clock in the hall. "Did you just shave?"

"What makes you think so?"

I reached up to lift a smudge of shaving cream off his earlobe and showed him the evidence. "I'm honing my sleuthing eye for detail. Plus, it's three in the morning and you, who should be in your pj's, reek of Old Spice."

Both his earlobes turned bright red. *Guilty.* But of what?

"Well," my father said, slipping his hands in the pockets of his well-worn smoking jacket, "I could say I'm going to school early today."

"It's Sunday."

"I'm waiting for the morning paper?"

I might once have been the ten-year-old mother figure in this family, but I'd had this dear man, this knight in shining armor, at my back—or should I say his shoulder beneath my cheek. "Lucky for you, your Old Spice still makes the little girl in me want to crawl into your lap so you can make all my problems go away."

"A daughter may outgrow your lap, but she will never outgrow your heart," he said, slipping an arm around me. "Author unknown."

"I love you, Dad." I kissed his cheek and wished I could ease his burdens as effortlessly as he'd once eased mine. I also wished I had time to process the mystery of his middle-of-the-night shave.

Our neighbors had probably already reported us for

disturbing the peace, and I had a vision of cop cars filling our drive. Again.

I opened the door to a woman I'd never seen before—though her features superimposed themselves on my frightful memory of a corpse—a doppelgänger who about made me jump from my skin: a dead girl, alive again.

Breathing hard and trembling on my doorstep. A fashionista with a full set—all eleventy-seven pieces—of Louis Vuitton luggage; a clone, scared, embarrassed, hopeful. "Are you *the* Madeira Cutler? The one who worked for Faline? Brandy said you'd be here."

Another reminder of Brandy's effect on the household at large. "I'm Maddie Cutler. May I ask who you are?"

"Of course. Well." The woman seemed lost as she fumbled to explain. "This is the right address. Let me start from the beginning."

"I'd be grateful."

"Someone stole my purse with my train ticket and paycheck in it—must cave and choose direct deposit. My assets are frozen because somebody tried to clean out my account. So I had to report the break-in to the police, which took forever, then I didn't have the cash to take a train or the time to get money from relatives, so I borrowed a few dollars and got a ride from a friend . . . or five. Sorry I'm so late."

"Late for what?" I asked. Could I still be dreaming? Subconsciously turning back time?

"Late for the job as your intern, of course. You still want me, don't you?"

"That depends. Who are you?"

"Isobel York. Brandy said you were expecting me."

"I had been, but . . . something . . . made me think you weren't coming." I looked at my father. "Dad, you wanna call Lytton? I'll speed-dial Nick."

"Got it," he said, raising his cell phone and walking down the hall into the ladies' parlor to talk on the phone in private.

I slipped my phone from my pocket. A simple "Get over here," did it for Nick. He didn't care why.

Meanwhile, our front door stood open, our middle-of-the-night caller wilting on the front stoop.

Did I believe her foolish story? If the dead girl had been wearing this outfit, I would never have doubted her identity. Isobel York Two sported a sixties short-sleeved tent dress in beige, the neck and single pleat both piped in black, with a single black frog closure across the pleat at the bodice. Beauty in simplicity. She carried a simple black patent clutch to go with her sixties slingback pumps.

That's why I *should* believe her story. She dressed the part. But seriously, one could as easily hide beneath an outfit as make a splash and be "seen" in it.

I hated keeping her on the stoop.

I hated the thought of letting her inside.

"May I come in?" fashion-plate Isobel asked, and I

feared it wasn't safe to say yes. I mean, she was posing as a dead girl. That had to be some kind of offense, though I didn't know how you could arrest someone for having a dead person's face.

Identical. The word I'd spoken earlier today reverberated in my mind as I selected and tossed scenarios. Maybe in the light of day, she would be—a dead ringer. I winced at my mental pun too late to edit my thoughts, their poor taste notwithstanding.

Obviously tired, she leaned against the doorjamb and folded her arms. "Did you get Grand-mère's trunk?"

The word "trunk" hit me like a suction cup–tipped arrow between the eyes.

I mentally yanked it off my brow, imagining a cartoonish "slurp" so I'd have time to form an answer.

"Madeira," my father said, "she hasn't pulled a gun on us; I think we can let her inside until the police get here."

"Police?" our visitor asked, though she seemed grateful to accept the chair my father offered in our keeping room, first room off the front hall, to the right, across from the kitchen, and about two feet from the front door.

I took the chair across the table from her. "This will come as a surprise to you," I told her, "but someone else came to town today, with *your* wallet and driver's license."

"Oh. So you doubt I'm me? That explains your reaction. Sorry I can't prove who I am, unless . . . Did you look at the label on Grand-mère's trunk?"

"I did, when I thought you weren't coming and I considered sending it back."

"So you saw you couldn't because the return address is this address, right? Who else would know that? Other than the person who addressed it?"

"True." I sure wished the cavalry would get here. I wanted to keep the imposter talking—maybe she'd incriminate herself—except that I was beginning to like her. If only she didn't remind me of a certain corpse.

My father set down a cup of hot chocolate in front of her. Thoughtful man.

"Thank you, Mr. Cutler. At least, I assume you're Brandy's father. I didn't borrow enough money to eat dinner."

My dad crossed to the kitchen, again and came back a few minutes later with a cheese sandwich and a plate of Aunt Fee's famous cinnamon rolls.

I whipped my gaze his way as he straightened the logs in the basket beside the keeping room's people-tall fireplace, complete with cast-iron kettle and built-in brick oven.

"Did Aunt Fiona come home and stay long enough to bake?"

"No, she left enough frozen buns to keep me supplied until she gets home," he admitted, entirely too focused on his task.

I rubbed my face with a hand and released a sigh. How could he *not* know how Aunt Fiona felt about him? Worse, how could he not know how *he* felt about her?

"Feel better?" I asked the stranger after she'd inhaled the sandwich and a cinnamon bun.

I followed our guest's surprised gaze and saw Nick standing by the front stairs, watching us.

"Nick! Did you climb up the getaway tree instead of coming to the front door?"

"Call me crazy, but I just assumed, when you said 'Get over here' at this hour . . . Evening, Mr. Cutler."

My father gave Nick his most professorial expression of disapproval. Sore subject, the getaway tree outside Brandy's room. Every one of Dad's four children got caught at one time or another sneaking a *special* friend in or out that way.

Nick had his eye on that last cinnamon bun, but our visitor picked it up, so I presume that he went into the kitchen for another.

Werner knocked twice and walked in. "Late nights are getting to be a habit," he said.

I swallowed hard, fast, and wrong, and about coughed up a lung. Good thing I'd told Nick we'd had dinner a few times.

"Too late to be shy," Werner said, sounding a bit like the grammar school brat who'd provoked me into calling him Little Wiener.

"Shush," I said.

"You don't have pepper spray or a Taser on you, do you?" he asked. "Tear gas? A grenade in your pocket?

You're making me nervous," Werner said, so focused on me, he hadn't yet noticed my father or our visitor.

"Good evening, Detective," my father said, stretching to his full height from the fireplace behind my chair. "Has my daughter been terrorizing you?"

"Since the first time I saw her."

"That makes two of us," Nick said as he reentered the room, eating a cinnamon roll.

Werner did a double take, then he recaptured his equilibrium. "Heard you were on your way, Jaconetti. Welcome home."

The detective turned back to me. "What's the rush that couldn't wait until morning?"

"You might not have noticed that we have a visitor," I said, indicating our midnight caller, seated out of range.

Werner turned his head, stilled, then leaned my way. "Cadaver clone, twelve o'clock."

"Uh, yeah. That's why I called."

"Leave it to me, kiddo. I'll protect you."

Nick cleared his throat.

Nine

Clothes can suggest, persuade, connote, insinuate, or indeed lie, and apply subtle pressure while their wearer is speaking frankly and straightforwardly of other matters.

—ANNE HOLLANDER

Our doppelgänger stood, all five feet eight or nine of her, in classic vintage—though her Manolo Blahnik booties were very today at about eight hundred-plus dollars. She was in her mid-twenties, dark hair and doe eyes, looked a little lost, a lot frazzled, uncomfortable in her surroundings, at the mercy of strangers, and trying not to reveal her panic to the odd lot of us.

That I sensed it, I blamed on my years as New York fashion designer Faline's first assistant when I worked with newbie runway models. Now, that was a lesson in hidden panic.

Also, panic had become a frequent visitor of mine since I got my first psychometric reading.

"If you didn't want me to work for you, Ms. Cutler,"

our visitor said, her perfect chin rising, her pride a bit of a sham, "you should have said so right away. And, Detective, I don't appreciate the name-calling. Cadaver clone? Am I so pale I look dead to you? Frankly, I went through hell after having my purse ransacked."

"A lot of that going around today," I said. "Can you ID your mugger?"

"No mugger. A thief. In my apartment. But still, even after losing my ID, money, and train ticket, I busted my buttress to get here on time. So I don't appreciate being made to feel like a two-headed giraffe in Gucci at a Quant exhibit."

"Now that's what I call a fashion intern," I said, impressed by the accuracy in her statement. I mean, who else would know Mary Quant, inventor of the miniskirt, these days, except a student of fashion? And just look at the way she's dressed.

"I meant no offense," Werner said. "Miss Cutler and I speak with a kind of shorthand. We've been, ah, frenemies, since third grade. I'm Detective Lytton Werner, by the way," he said, offering his hand. "And you are?"

"Isobel York."

Werner did a double take, gawked, and shut his mouth, though it fell open again. Still, he tried to compose himself, too late. "Was anything besides your purse stolen from your apartment?" he asked.

"Actually, my Coach purse was found in the stairs

outside my apartment, for which I thank the stars, since it cost an arm and a hoof."

"A giraffe hoof, one presumes?" Werner said. "Can you come down to the station in the morning so we can get your fingerprints?"

I silently questioned the weird request with a look.

"You were right this morning," he said. "Peach peasant blouse and socks do not a *correct* identification make, not for a fashionista."

Could our middle-of-the-night visitor conceivably *be* Ms. York, in the flesh, then? "The resemblance *is* uncanny," I said.

"Resemblance to who and fingerprints why?" Isobel asked, looking from one of us to the other. "*I* didn't steal anything."

"No," I said, making the save, "but if your wallet is found, they'll need to know which prints are yours." If Isobel was related to the deceased—which she certainly appeared to be—we couldn't break the news until we confirmed the relationship.

"I was visiting family at my apartment in D.C. when I lost my wallet, actually, though I spend most of my time at my apartment in New York," Isobel said.

Werner made a note of that. "Can you tell us who knew you were coming here?"

"My friends, my family, and likely my father's workers, you know, the people who keep his family straight because he doesn't have time."

"Maybe we should save the third degree for daylight?" I suggested.

Werner turned to our guest. "If someone broke into your apartment before you left home," he said, taking notes, "that's a far cry from slipping a hand into your purse while you were, say, in the two-headed giraffe pen at the zoo."

"Very different," she said. "And yes, someone had to have broken into my apartment—no other way for my bag to get into the hall—but the D.C. police said there were no signs of forced entry. They think I might have left my door open."

"Where did you go without your purse?" Nick asked.

"To my neighbor's with my apartment key in my pocket. I know I had it, because I used it to lock my door."

"So," Nick said, "your intruder could have had a key and he/she *saw* you go to your neighbor's?"

Isobel tilted her head, considering the possibility.

I sat beside her. "Have you ever given anyone a spare key?"

"My sister used to live with me, but she moved to Los Angeles ages ago, and she lost her key. She certainly didn't need it once she moved."

"I'll touch base with the D. C. police," Werner said. "Can you describe your sister?"

"You're looking at her. We're twins. Identical, though my father always called her the wild one. I don't know;

I felt pretty wild today trying to get friends and friends of friends to tag-team me here."

Werner cleared his throat, as if he had final say. "I'm going to ask you not to leave town tonight, Ms. York. Do you have a place to stay?"

"I thought I did, but . . . may I sleep in jail? I'll get Grand-mère to wire me some money in the morning."

My head came up. "I thought your grandmother was dead."

"Grand-mère? You mean, because I gave you her trunk of vintage clothes? No, she gave the trunk to my twin, who gave it to me. She said it contained bad memories but great clothes. Things a fashion plate would appreciate. Aren't they awesome?"

"I didn't open the trunk. I . . . guess I was waiting for you."

My father checked his watch and stood up. "Miss York, you're welcome to move in as planned."

"I don't advise it, Mr. Cutler," Werner said, "unless you have a room for me, too."

"And me," Nick said, a familiar twinkle in his eyes. "I'll take Brandy's room."

"No, Isobel will have the room across from mine. This was a tavern," I added. "We have room enough for the entire force."

"Am I under arrest?" Isobel asked.

"No," I assured her. "Call it protective custody. I

think we might have seen your twin today, and let's say for now that she's in a bit of trouble."

"Listen, her full name is Giselle Trouble York. She'll worm her way out of whatever she got herself into, though. Trust me."

"But can you trust her to keep you out of trouble?" I asked. "What if the wrong person thinks you're her?"

Isobel's shoulders sagged. "Great point!"

We all looked up when the doorbell rang.

My father opened it to Aunt Fiona, fresh off the plane, if her wheeled suitcase was any indication.

"Wow," she said. "Welcome by *committee*, I didn't expect. Although I should have known when I saw Nick's and the detective's cars out front."

Aunt Fee had expected a committee of one, judging by her barely veiled disappointment. A lot like my dad's badly hidden longing.

I turned to Werner, and my heart about stopped, because I saw the same look on his face, except he was looking at me. Ack! "Friends," I said, nodding. "We're all friends now. You and me, me and Nick, you and Nick. 'Kay?"

"You sure?" Werner asked. "I don't like that he hurt you."

"All's forgiven. God knows you and I have forgiven each other enough times."

Werner ran his hand through his hair. "Well, that's true."

"We have to talk!" Nick said, looking from Werner to me and back to the detective, narrowing his eyes. "I think that my case and your case have their tentacles around each other's throats. Upstairs. Now!"

"You bet," Werner said, setting me physically aside.

"Hey!" I called after them. "Wait. Nick, what you just said? Is that code for 'I'm gonna whop your ascot'?"

"Why would he do that?" Werner asked me. "We're all friends, right?"

"Are you kidding? Is this some show of testosterone for my benefit?"

"Don't worry, ladybug," Nick said, turning on the stairs. "It's about the case."

"Mad, I'll take care of it," Werner said, agreeing with Nick, which made me feel a bit better.

"But I want to be involved in the case, Nick. You said to get proactive."

"Proactive in your own special way," my former boy toy said, he who knew me better than I knew myself.

Werner nodded his agreement. "Nick's right. This is preliminary stuff. Doesn't concern you. Not yet."

"The hell it doesn't!" What the Hermès were they up to? Did they intend to discuss the case? Or me?

Nick led the way upstairs, and Werner followed.

I slammed my hand on the newel post. "Stubborn idiots!"

My father chuckled. "'Daughters are like flowers;

they fill the world with beauty, and sometimes attract pests.' Author unknown. Smart, but unknown."

Isobel stood. "Do you give fathering lessons? My dad never said anything half as sweet or clever. If he did, he would have said it at the most inappropriate time."

"My father's an English professor at UConn," I said. "A quote for every occasion, hey, Dad? Aunt Fee, may I have the key to your house? I don't want to see either of those traitors when they come down. We're all friends, now, so they cut me out of the conversation? I don't think so."

"I don't blame you," Isobel said.

"You're coming with me," I told her.

My father cleared his throat. "Half an hour ago, you didn't want to let her into the house, Mad."

"Well, call me Groucho Marx, but she said the secret word: Mary Quant. Only a fashionista could have made such an easy statement. Plus she knew the return address on the trunk was this address."

"I guess we've sort of bonded," Isobel said. "And I'm glad, because I want to hear more about those two upstairs. They're both in love with you, boss. You know that, right?"

My father chuckled. "She knows it."

I rolled my eyes. Maybe I did know it, but I wasn't ready to "hear" it. "Dad, may Aunt Fee sleep here, tonight?" I asked, trying not to grin. "And can you tell my friends, Detective Dickaroo and the Bumburglar, that I expect a full report of their discussion tomorrow?"

"Sure," my father said. "Anything for you, sweetheart."

Watching him and Fee, I chuckled. I couldn't help myself. "I may be your daughter, but I'm neither dumb nor two years old. You want us out, and fast."

Aunt Fee made so bold as to hook her arm through my father's.

He blustered, but when she covered his hand with hers, he didn't protest or remove it. He laced their fingers together.

I winked at him. "Tell Werner that Isobel and I will see him at the station at some point tomorrow morning."

The escalating discussion upstairs made me drag Isobel and her overnight bag out the door.

Ten

Fashion contains the potential for renewal and transformation. The more costumes one has, the more fantasy personas one can adopt.

—EDITH GOULD

"I'll take Aunt Fiona's room," I told Isobel on arrival. Because I felt responsible for Aunt Fiona's things. "And you can have the guest room." Since guest rooms by nature held nothing of personal worth.

"Ms. Cutler, what should I call you?"

"Not Madeira. Mostly people call me that if they're angry with me or they're my father. How about Maddie?"

"How about boss?" she suggested. "I'd be more comfortable."

I'd feel weird. "Sure, go for it. It's a new one, but at least it doesn't make me feel like a bottle of wine."

"Okay, boss."

"You're not gonna believe it," Isobel said, coming out of the guest room a short while later. "I packed so much makeup, I forgot my nightshirt."

"We have a lot in common. No problem. Aunt Fiona has some fun sleepwear we can raid."

Isobel sat on Aunt Fee's bed. "Why didn't your aunt come home with us?"

"Her and my dad have a non-relationship she's trying to turn around."

"Your dad's nuts about her. Seriously, he got all choked up when she got there. I thought they were lovers."

"My father is so thick. Even you, a stranger, can see what he can't."

"Your aunt doesn't deny her feelings," Isobel remarked as I laid out some of my favorite witch-humor nightwear.

"Fee's not actually related to us. She was my mom's best friend in college, and she's been there for us always, and especially since we lost Mom twenty years ago. Here," I said with a flourish. "Take your pick."

"Um, is your non-aunt a witch, by any chance?"

"What gave her away?" I asked on a chuckle. My shorty red sleep shirt said, Save a Broom, Ride a Witch.

Isobel checked hers in the mirror. In turquoise her sleep tee warned: Beware the Naughty Witch Inside. "Too bad we'll only get to wear them a couple of hours." Isobel chuckled. "When do we need to be at the police station?"

"Since tomorrow is Sunday, and I don't open the shop until ten, let's get a whole four hours' sleep." She'd need her rest, I thought, because she very well might discover tomorrow that her twin had been murdered. The least I could do was give her a blissfully ignorant good night's slumber. "Maybe I'll call Werner in the morning and tell him if he wants to fingerprint you, he can come to the shop. He'll love that."

"I've only known him for an hour, and already, I know he'll hate it."

"Yeah, well, that'll be my perk."

She chuckled. "Do you think your aunt will mind if I shower? It's been a hot and sweaty day. You know, for a while there, we thought somebody was following us."

"That's disturbing," I said. "The thought of some-body following, I mean, not the shower. Go for it. You'll sleep better."

I'd turned down both our beds and was making cham-omile tea, not a little worried about the possibility that Isobel had been followed, when I thought I heard some-one outside in the bushes near the front door, so I went toward the living room and stopped, stunned, when I saw the doorknob turn.

I turned off the lights, grabbed a hefty rose quartz owl from a nearby shelf, and leaned against the wall beside the door, owl raised, heart pumping about thirty beats over the speed limit.

When the door opened, I owled the intruder upside

the head. Crack. He went down like a California sequoia, and though his partner caught me around the waist, I swung my arm up and owled him beneath the chin, the louder crack making me a little sick.

The room flooded with light. Isobel stood with her hand on the switch. "Remind me never to cross you. I mean, I know they excluded you from their discussion at your dad's, but—"

"What?" I looked down at my assailants. "Nick? Werner? Oh my God, they're gonna bleed all over Aunt Fee's white rug."

I sat Nick up. "How's your jaw, sweetie?" I tried to cup it.

He eyed me. "Schweww. Schwell," he pronounced more carefully the second time. "Ow."

Scrap. "You might have a little jaw damage, there."

Isobel got Werner sitting up. "Maddie, the detective has a knot and a half on his head."

"Ice packs!" I ordered, and she ran. "Hmm. She might make a good intern after all."

The men in my life eyed me, like, well, maybe I should put the owl back where it belonged.

I did so. "Guys, you could have called my name, introduced yourselves, something, before walking in. Frankly, when I saw that doorknob turn, all I could think of was Isobel's threatening caller and her fear of being followed today. I did what I had to, to protect her."

They nodded like I made a certain sense.

I put my fists on my hips. "Now what the hell are you doing *here*?"

I looked from one of them to the other. "You beat the scrap out of each other, didn't you? Who won?"

They each pointed to themselves.

"I thought you were discussing the case," I said.

Werner cleared his throat. "We got, er, sidetracked."

Nick pointed at Werner, like the detective got it right, and Werner wagged his finger and nodded enthusiastically, like I should pay attention.

"Yeah, that," I muttered.

"The upshot was that Nick and I both vowed not to hurt you."

"Fancy that," I said, touched, and my need to annihilate them became a shot of the warm fuzzies. Pity, I'd already beat the scrap out of them.

Werner took the ice packs from Isobel, held one to his head and one to his purple eye. "I'm here to protect Isobel," he said.

"Why?" Isobel asked.

Nick leaned on an elbow and held his jaw, looking at me like a hungry puppy. "Iiisssth?"

"Oh, ice. Isobel, two more ice packs."

"Think you broke something?" I asked Nick, horrified.

He pointed at me.

"I broke something?"

71

Nick shrugged, got off the floor, sat on a sofa, and gratefully accepted the ice packs.

Werner sat beside him.

"Matching black eyes. Man, I wish I had a camera. Oh, wait." I used my camera phone. *Click!* "For posterity . . . and blackmail." I showed it to Isobel.

She nodded. "That'd make a fine Christmas card."

I shoved her arm. "We're gonna get along great!"

Nick moved to the sofa opposite.

"Too late," I said. "So, Nick, if Werner's here to protect Isobel, who are you here to protect?"

Again, he pointed to me.

"From who?"

Nick glared at Werner.

Isobel giggled. "They were fighting over *you*? Go, boss."

"We're friends. Just friends. I think we should take them to the hospital."

The ice pack club denied the need with mutinous looks.

"Isobel, go get some sleep. I'll stay up and keep Werner busy so he doesn't fall asleep, in the event he has a concussion."

Nick's head came up, and he gave Werner the evil eye. "No sweep. No anysing." He was, of course, referring to the night of Werner's concussion when we shared that thermonuclear kiss.

I sat beside Werner, and Nick growled. "Oh, for pity's

sake. I need to make sure Werner's pupils aren't dilated."

"I think they are," Werner said.

Nick narrowed his eyes at the two of us, and if black looks were darts . . .

Eleven

Clothing should be used as a tool and as a weapon.
—JOHN T. MOLLOY

"Boy, I hate to do this," Werner whispered, practically kissing my ear, so I pretended to be half-asleep; then he moved me away from him, lowered me so my head rested on the sofa pillow instead of his shoulder. He stood and covered me with Aunt Fee's Irish knit afghan.

Both of us checked on Nick, asleep, half sitting up, looking hunky dishy, to tell the truth, and I feared that someday I might be forced to choose between them. How could I be half in lust with both of them?

"Thanks, Lytton," I said, yawning, too tired to figure it out. Time would surely tell.

The scent of coffee and pancakes woke me at about the same time as Nick. "Where's Werner?" he asked.

"I have no idea."

"He's been cooking," Isobel said, handing us each a cup of coffee. "With me."

Gee, I got a little jealous lurch at that, then I remembered him tucking me in last night, and I smiled and sipped my coffee.

We sat at Fee's glass-topped table overlooking the deck and the Mystic River beyond, and Werner came in with a platter of pancakes for us, and oatmeal thinned with applesauce for Nick.

"You both look like scrap," I said. "And you're both gonna say you beat the scrap out of each other, aren't you?"

Two firm nods.

"What are you going to say you were fighting over?" Isobel asked, her fork halfway to her mouth.

Nick set down his spoon and stood. "Dentith," he said, and left, slamming the door behind him.

"Thanks for the help cleaning up," I called after him. Once the three of us erased any sign of our presence, Werner went home to change with a promise from us that we'd meet him at the station later.

Isobel and I drove back to my father's to get dressed.

Like a fashion week show-and-tell, she opened her Vuitton cases, every piece, and I opened my walk-in closet, once a spare room. And like filings to magnets, the two of us gravitated toward each other's vintage collections.

As it happened, Isobel fell for my form-fitting two-tone empire dress, bottom a dark taupe, top, black with cap sleeves, maker unknown. And over it, the matching bolero, known these days as a shrug.

I chose her navy, two-piece sailor suit dress with a pencil skirt and short-sleeved top. The square notched collar piped in white had a smaller collar atop a larger one, with a red star embroidered at each corner.

Isobel went into the bathroom, and I into my closet dressing room to try on our chosen outfits. As soon as I slipped an arm into the dress, I realized I'd underestimated the power in my psychic gift, simply because it hadn't appeared in so long.

With the sailor dress wrapped around my shoulders, one arm sleeved, the other free, I sank to my dressing room floor, landing with a thud on my mother's favorite old Oriental carpet.

My closet disappeared, and I hovered over a docked three-masted sailboat.

A girl wearing the same dress as me, one who looked like Isobel, headed toward port, or starboard—who knew?

She hesitated when she saw a man posed, not quite tall nor lean, against the rail with his back to her, his hair a dull nutmeg color.

He held his left hand so as to show off a diamond the size of his ego. The emerald cut beauty was set deep in a bright, very pure gold, a calling card and a pickup line all in one.

Here was a man who needed props. I had his number, though I'd yet to see his face. I watched the woman who'd worn this dress at some point previous to me.

"I trust you had a good flight, Carissima?" the man said without turning.

Had she flown in to meet him? Where from? I wondered.

The boat began to move, and I sensed a rising panic from the girl, worse than from any psychometric vision ever.

"There she is," said Flimflam Man, though the character analysis was a guess on my part. "The Golden Gate Bridge," he said. "Today Sausalito; tomorrow, I'll take you to Napa. A weekend to remember, one well worth your price. Whether I'm buying, *like now*, or selling, when necessary, I always get value for someone's money, my costly one, and you'll like this part: I always leave my ladies wanting more."

Ducky for Isobel . . . or her twin.

Why did he not turn to her but continue to stare out to sea, keeping his back to her, even as they conversed?

Meanwhile, she trembled visibly, and I wished I knew why.

"What shall I call you?" he asked her. "You may call me Gian or Carlo, or *mi amore*. And I will call you Bella Carissima, no?"

No! I thought.

"*Sí*, Gian," his hired date said too submissively to be

my new intern. But how well did I know Isobel after only a few hours?

His hired date finally stepped to the rail beside him, and Gian turned to face her, raising his glasses at the same time.

When she screamed, I wished I could make out more than the partial silhouette of a man whose glasses reflected the sun, obliterating his face.

"It is you!" she said, stepping back. "How can you afford all this? Are you skimming off the top?"

He gave her a rather sick smile. "What do you care? I know your dirty little secret. A call girl." He chuckled. "I always wanted something priceless to hold over the old boy."

"He won't believe you. Not about me. But he will believe my boss when she tells him about you."

"Madam C?" He scoffed. "Oh, she's a reliable source."

I wished I knew the name of the call girl. Maybe I should have been treating my potential intern less like a friend and more like a suspect—not that a call girl would automatically be a suspect, except that the two of them were talking blackmail.

Logically speaking, I should probably have treated Isobel more formally, like an employee, though yesterday's threatening morning caller practically put a target on her back, so protecting her made sense.

"Isn't this the bomb?" Isobel asked, no longer on the boat—if she had ever been on the boat—but in my dressing room doorway looking gorgeous in my two-tone empire dress with a pencil skirt.

"Oh, did you pass out?" she asked as she helped me up.

"Guess I didn't eat enough breakfast." I slipped my free arm in the sleeve of her sailor dress, buttoned the top, and smoothed the fitted skirt on my hips.

She stood back and nodded. "You look splendid."

Who are you, Isobel York? I wondered. If you are Isobel York.

The girl on the sailboat seemed better suited to being a call girl than a model and fashion designer, though supposedly Isobel only modeled for Madame Robear to put herself through fashion design school. Good call, because she had fashionista written all over her.

What had Brandy gotten me into this time?

I should keep it on a business level between us until the case was solved, I thought, but I'd look like a jerk if I backed away from this friendly dress trade. What would it hurt if Isobel and I wore each other's clothes for one day? I could back away bit by bit after. Turn myself into the boss and her into the intern.

Piece of cake.

"Wanna trade handbags, too?" she asked, clapping her hands.

Uh . . . "Sure." Man, she was riding for a fall. I really didn't want her to have to view the body at the morgue.

We traded box bags by Will Hardy, or Wilardy, as he often signed them. I chose a white swirl-pearl hatbox-shaped Lucite bag with two handles that tilted toward each other after a twist and turn and met at the center top.

She fell for my caramel-colored Lucite, maker unknown, shaped like a man's lunchbox, circa 1950s, all the way to its single handle.

Despite my short, weird sail on San Francisco Bay, I admitted to a bad case of purse envy.

Having found a kindred fashionista in Isobel, I worried more by the minute about her reaction to yesterday's events. The dead girl must be her twin.

That also could have been her twin on the boat. Giselle Trouble York. Too bad Gian hadn't used her real name.

When Isobel went back into my bathroom, I texted Werner. "Be there soon. Find Isobel's twin."

His reply came too fast. "I think we have her."

Scrap. I put more play in our preparation by opening my hat closet, putting off the inevitable, and yes, letting her know, albeit subtly, that I'd be there for her. So much for treating her like a suspect.

Already, I was going against my vow to put distance between us. True, I'm a pushover, though I can only be pushed so far.

Isobel lost her breath when she saw my hat closet and approached it like the Sistine Chapel. Shh. Sacred place.

She chose a sienna skullcap with a tan-flowered black band. Perfect with her dress.

I found a natural sisal straw hat with a short brim and a red grosgrain ribbon. A match for a sailor suit.

Shoes: We wore the same size, though she had a higher arch and me, a narrower foot, but at least 80 percent of our considerable shoe collections would fit us both.

She wore my tan and black vintage Diors, and I squeaked, drooled, lusted, and slipped my feet into her 1920s Maud Frizon navy Mary Janes with white piping and squash heels. "I'd kill for these," I said, trying not to wince at the horrific statement.

We should be going to an amusement park. We'd dressed more for fun than—

"Boss, you look like somebody walked on your grave."

How had I let this turn into playing dress-up? "Let's go before Werner comes looking for us."

"I like your car," she said getting in a few minutes later. "Did I say that last night? It's awfully pretty in daylight."

"Thanks. You look gorgeous," I said as I drove.

"I'm looking forward to meeting your customers," she said, "after we see your cute detective."

"Werner's not exactly mine."

"Don't tell him that. He never stopped talking about you while he made breakfast."

"Really? Did he tell you what I called him in third grade, in front of the whole school?"

"He did, as if he was proud of you. He said it was the making of him. He said Nick *used* to be yours, like since junior high. He stressed the past tense."

As I turned into the station parking lot, I had a sick feeling we were going to be stressing the past a lot this morning.

Twelve

Good design is a renaissance attitude that combines technology, cognitive science, human need, and beauty to produce something that the world didn't know it was missing.

—PAOLA ANTONELLI

I stopped Isobel in the parking lot. "Whatever happens, you're not alone, okay?"

"What could happen?"

"Well, I hope, nothing," I said. "But just know that I wanted you to have a good night's sleep, so there was no point in playing what-if last night."

Isobel frowned. "Okaaay."

I took her arm. "Let's go. I'm here for you."

"You're scaring the cotton batting out of me."

"Sorry."

Werner, rising from the chair at his desk when we went into his office, looked like he went twenty rounds with Bigfoot.

"Tut, tut, tut, Detective," I said. "Your face is a forest of greens and blues."

Isobel commiserated with him. "But that's an especially great shade of teal," she said.

"Thanks, both of you, I think. I ran into a steel fist then a curvaceous yet surprisingly lean, mean, feisty machine." He furrowed his brows. "You think I look ghastly? Not handsome or studly?"

I chuckled. "Your eye looks ghastly. The rest of you is . . . passable."

"Stop. I might die of embarrassment." He came from around his desk and took my arm. "Miss York," he said, turning to Isobel. "Please take a seat, and somebody will be right with you. I need to chide our saucy Ms. Cutler, where no one will hear us, if you get my drift."

Isobel's eyes twinkled as she sat, but she bit her lip as if she remembered our parking lot conversation.

Two men passed us on our way out of Werner's office, a suave, buff, leader type wearing a navy pinstripe wool silk Armani with a cream silk shirt and an emerald silk tie.

Behind him followed a man with rusty hair, shorter, broader, but appearing full of his own worth, his tan suit of good quality but made by a less prestigious designer. I looked back at him twice, before Werner urged me forward. Something about him intrigued me.

Together, they went into Werner's office, and Rusty shut the door behind them, like he was in charge.

I did a double take, wondering why Werner would let two strangers close themselves in with— "Those guys just went into your office. Don't you care?"

"Sure I do."

"But Isobel's in there. Maybe one is the fake-voiced bully who kept calling the shop terrorizing me and asking for her."

"You didn't say your caller *terrorized* you."

"I was sure I did last night. And I told you when it happened that he spoke through a voice changer, which made him sound like Vader with a bullhorn, and . . . he had a tone."

"Well, then." Werner steered me in an unexpected direction. "Billings, throw the book at anybody with a deep voice . . . and a tone."

"You're mocking me."

"You should know. You could win a Pulitzer for mockery; you could teach mockery as an alternative to swordplay or knife throwing. Turn it into an Olympic sport."

I raised a brow. "So you're saying I'm sharp-witted?"

"Sharp-tongued. Vast difference."

"I'll show you the difference," I snapped.

He scanned the nearly empty squad room and lowered his voice. "Please do."

"Meanwhile, Isobel could be getting accosted by a couple of strangers."

"The dark suit is Mr. Quincy York, Isobel and

Giselle's father, who is running for first selectman of Kingston's Vineyard. I'm counting on him to identify the girl he's talking to and settling the question as to whether she's your intern or not.

"The tan suit is his campaign manager/right-hand man, Mr. Ruben Rickard. I'll introduce you after they finish their talk. Listen to their voices, would you? And tell me if either of them is your caller."

I cupped Werner's chin. "Voice mod-u-la-tor. To decipher that, I think we'd need a wiretap and a techno geek.

"What the hell is going on here?" I asked, dead-ended in a secluded corner.

"Mr. Rickard identified the dead girl as Mr. Quincy York's niece, Isobel's first cousin, Payton. They're about to tell Isobel—or Giselle—about her first cousin."

"I'm so relieved that Isobel didn't lose her twin, but I'm confused, too. Why get a second ID?"

"We didn't seek it out. *Before* Isobel arrived last night, we called Mr. York to inform him of Isobel's death, per Ms. Robear's ID. York and Rickard showed up today, because we didn't know, before Isobel told us last night, that she had an identical twin. Rickard viewed the body and told us we made a mistake. It's not one of York's daughters but his brother Patrick's daughter. York was as surprised as we were—and his relief perfunctory— that Robear gave us a bad ID."

"No fingerprint confirmation?"

"No fingerprints on record for any of the three girls anywhere."

"Okay, so why did Rickard and not York view the body?"

"Evidently, Rickard does all York's dirty work."

"Oh." I scrunched my brows and shook my head. "Still confused. How could Payton look so much like her cousins?"

Werner urged me down the hall, back toward the squad room. "Isobel's father and his brother, Patrick, married twin sisters. They say the three girls only look alike to the untrained eye."

"I wonder if Isobel ever loaned Payton her sailor dress."

"What?"

"Nothing." Could Payton have been the girl on the sailboat in San Francisco Bay?

"She sure didn't dress like a York for her train ride yesterday," I said. "She must have been in disguise."

"You're right. Rickard was appalled when he saw the clothes she'd been wearing. He said they weren't hers."

I couldn't believe I was thinking this, but if I could get my hands on them . . . I shuddered. "I assume her clothes are still being held as evidence?"

"Absolutely. Why? Do you want a look at them?"

Not in front of him, I didn't. "Maybe when they're released from evidence, in case Isobel wants them. Did both brothers have twins? I mean, is Payton a twin?"

"No. The twins have one cousin, Payton, our deceased, born about a week after Isobel and Giselle."

"Have you located Giselle?"

"She seems to be a happy wanderer. She's not at the York family home or at her L.A., New York, Aspen, or Palm Springs condos. Her father hasn't seen her in six months; but that doesn't seem to be unusual for him."

"That's a lot of condos." Gee, who could afford so many homes? I don't know. Maybe a . . . very high-end call girl?

"I know," Werner said. "We're looking into her financials, too."

"Have other family members seen her?"

"None we've talked to, which takes our investigation up a notch."

"As in, Giselle's a suspect? Or she's dead somewhere, too?"

Werner nodded. "She could be a suspect, but I'm also concerned about her welfare. We've issued a national missing persons bulletin. I'm still talking to Isobel's father. I don't know if either set of parents is still married, if any of the three girls lived with their parents. I'd know more if you hadn't shown up so early. I was in the middle of asking Candidate York a few questions."

"I wish you'd told me last night to come in later. I'd have given Isobel more time to sleep this morning, though I think you woke her up with your loud cooking."

"I didn't wake *you* up, and I didn't expect my staff's investigative phone calls to net us a visit from Mr. Quincy York."

"Why is he such a big deal?"

"Highly publicized political aspirations," Werner said, "though he's definitely starting at the bottom. Famous family money."

"Ah. So famous I don't know him."

"You hate politics."

"Oh yeah. Madame Robear sure got it wrong. You'd think the owner of a modeling agency would know her models well enough to identify their faces correctly."

"You'd think." Werner turned to Billings, his sometimes driver, sometimes desk clerk. "Knock on this door when the people in my office come out."

Billings saluted and tried to hide his grin by focusing on his computer keys, as Werner backed me into a supply closet, hands on my upper arms, and kicked the door shut behind us.

"Are you seeking revenge?" I asked, coming up against a set of shelves.

"Maybe. See, I got this knot on the back of my head . . ."

He lowered his head to show me, his hands braced on the shelves behind me.

I combed my fingers through his hair until I found the bump. Couldn't miss it, really. High and hard, and wow, it must hurt. "It really is huge."

"I've dreamed of you saying that."

I shoved his shoulder. "You're a pain, but I apologize for knocking your lights out."

"You already apologized. Right before you fell asleep in my arms."

I gasped. "With Nick on the opposite sofa?"

"He passed out long before we did. Probably woke up yesterday in Timbuktu, secure in an assassin's trap, and then he came home to real trouble: you."

I kissed the knot I gave him. "Does that make it better?"

"Not as much as looking down your dress does."

I pulled his head up, his grin about cutting me off at the knees.

"Tell me you were *not* looking."

"Hey, this is you, kiddo. Of course I looked. You make a man's mouth water."

"I am not a pork chop!" Still, stupid me, my heart tripped.

He took my hand and ran his thumb over my fingernails. "You're all woman, Mad, especially in that yellow lace bra. I *like*. But I like what's inside better."

Inside me, he meant, not in my bra, right? Of course, right. "What are we doing here?" I asked. What was I doing here? Alone with the Wiener, and liking it?

"Testing the waters," he said. "Though with you, I always try to remember that drowning's a probability, and yet I forget. You're like some kind of bewitching sea siren. I've got the scars from where you've dashed me against the rocks. Yet here I am, ready for another dip. *Glug, glug, glug.*"

Thirteen

Clothes make a statement. Costumes tell a story.
—MASON COOLEY

Something that sounded like a paired set of sweat socks thumped against the supply room door. "Yo! Sarge!" A shout from Billings. "The people in your office are asking for you."

"Saved by the clerk," I said.

In Werner's office, I opened my arms to the girl her father confirmed as Isobel. "I'm sorry about your cousin. I didn't know."

"Of course you didn't," Isobel said, her eyes red. "Thank you."

Mr. York stood. "When can we expect to plan a service for my niece?" he asked, his lack of emotion disconcerting.

Werner sat behind his desk and moved a few things

around. An obvious stall. "As I told you earlier, we can't release . . . Payton . . . because we're waiting for a forensics report on cause of death."

Werner didn't tell Isobel's father that a suspicious caller kept asking about Isobel or that it was possible Payton made a bad choice in the identity she stole. I think he withheld as much as he could, because Mr. Quincy York seemed like a suspicious character himself. And I had a lot of questions about the campaign manager. I would have to draw Isobel out about her family as soon possible, because some things just didn't add up.

Werner clicked his pen. "In the meantime, we need answers, and you can help, Mr. York, by sitting down and giving me as many as possible."

Isobel and her father sat.

Werner checked his watch. "Mad, I know you need to open your shop. And, Ms. York, if it's all right with you, I'd rather speak to your father alone, so you can go with Ms. Cutler right now, if you don't mind. I'll stop by and talk to you at Mad's shop later, but you do need to stay in town until the investigation is over."

"I have to leave right away, Isobel," her father said. "You know that, right?"

"Yes, sir."

I exchanged a quick glance with Werner. "Isobel," he said, "stop by Billings's desk and get fingerprinted before you go."

"Why?" her father asked. "Surely you don't suspect Isobel of hurting her cousin?"

"If most people can't tell the three girls apart, it would behoove me to have a positive ID on at least two of them. It'll turn out to be proof that she *couldn't* have hurt her cousin. We had a chance to talk at breakfast. I think statements from the people who served as her tag-team taxis on her way here will give her an airtight alibi."

"Ah," Isobel said. "Then you'll know for sure that I'm me."

Mr. York frowned. "But you have my word."

And I thought, Nuff said.

Werner clicked his pen one more time.

"No problem, Daddy. Physical proof is good proof." She kissed her father's brow. "See you later. Call me when you're not busy with the campaign."

"I'll try," he said, appearing too preoccupied to grasp the concept. "Meanwhile," her father added, noticing she was still there, "you let Ruben here know if you need anything."

"Right." Isobel rolled her eyes and came my way.

Mr. York leaned toward Werner across the desk. "Is this a murder investigation?"

"We don't have cause of death for your niece, and that's all I can say right now."

"But she had my daughter's ID."

"Her license and train ticket. Yes, she did."

"And you say my other daughter is missing?"

"We are investigating Giselle's whereabouts. May we speak alone?" Werner asked, all detective now, recorder on, pen in hand, notebook open.

"Ruben, please wait for me in the squad room."

Ruben did as he was told.

I shut the door on Werner and Mr. York and turned to Isobel. "Mid-morning snack? Coffee?"

"No thanks."

"I'm sincerely sorry about your cousin. I don't mean to sound insensitive, but I need a Mint Mocha Chip Frappuccino. Sure you don't want one?"

"Make mine an Iced Caramel Macchiato, heavy on the caramel."

"That's my intern. You want Billings, here, for finger-printing, and I'll be right back."

Fifteen minutes later, Isobel waited for me outside the police station, trying to wear away her stained fin-gertips with a Wet-Nap.

She climbed into my Element with swollen eyes and a blotchy face. I was glad she'd released her emotions. I'd worried she was like her father and didn't have any.

"Is your dad still inside?" I asked, handing her the Macchiato.

"Either that or he left by the back door."

"You're close, then?"

"You give great snark," Isobel said. "I like that about you. Am I allowed to participate?"

"Yep, but we both pretend we're demure and ladylike in front of the customers."

"You're on, boss." She winked.

"Did anybody give you your wallet back?"

"No. Evidently, it's evidence. But your detective said he'd get me a duplicate license. What smells so good?"

"Warm brownies with thick, melty chocolate frosting."

"How do you stay so fit?"

"I don't have an elevator . . . except for caskets, but that's another story. I'll give you a tour of the shop when I have someone to watch the register, and you'll see why."

"I can't wait to explore Vintage Magic."

"I can't wait to open your grandmother's trunk."

"Brownies first, then the trunk," Isobel suggested. "I need a sugar rush, and you're in for a fashion rush when you look at Grand-mère's things."

"If you love your grand-mère's clothes so much, I think you should keep them as a memento of her."

"I don't want them, believe me."

"But we have the same taste. If I'll love the contents, then you must already adore them. We love the same things."

"Except for Grand-mère. We don't both love her."

I gave Isobel a double take. "Why don't we?

"She never liked me."

"Then why did she give you a *gorgeous* vintage trunk full of delicious vintage clothes?"

"She didn't. She gave them to Giselle. Gigi is every-body's fave. She's probably Daddy's sole heir, too."

"So why did Giselle give you the clothes if you don't get along?"

"It's not that we don't get along, we're just not friends. Don't you have a sibling you'd like to strangle more than the others?"

Brandy. "Right. Gotcha."

"Giselle doesn't like the bitter old lady any better than I do, and since I'm the fashionista in the family, she gave Grand-mère's clothes to me. Now I'm giving them to you."

"Were you friends with Payton?"

"Not especially, and I've been guilt-tripping about that since I found out she died."

"Who else doesn't like Payton?"

"Ask for the short list. Who liked her?"

"Okay, I'll bite. Who liked her?"

"Nobody I know."

"Not even your twin?"

"Especially not my twin."

"Payton's parents, then? They must have loved her."

"Not so much. Payton made sure of that."

Fourteen

The minute we walked toward the sitting area, Isobel went to the old black enamel undertaker's cabinet that I decorated. She traced the profile on the cabinet's side: a naked, fine-figured blonde standing on her toes at the bottom back, her head leaning toward the top front, as if peeking into the cabinet at my fashion doll collection inside.

Except for the curvaceous profile's long hair, black eyelashes, and red lips, I'd painted her an all-over flesh pink with no details.

"The design reminds me of a sixties Yves Saint Laurent wool jersey Pop Art dress."

"*That's* where I got the idea! You are so good. Nobody, but nobody who walks into this shop has ever connected that cabinet to, well, fashion design." I could stop worrying about her being Giselle posing as Isobel. This girl definitely studied fashion design. Isobel, for sure.

Yeah, her father's word just hadn't done it for me, but this did.

"I'm thrilled we speak the same language," Isobel said, sipping her Macchiato. "I love your art deco furniture, especially the sideboard."

"It was my mother's."

"Were the books hers, too? Or your aunt's? Love the titles. *Prince Smarmy: Boyfriends into Frogs and Other Fun Spells. How to Charm Your Way Out of a Bad Relationship. Mastering the Naughty Witch Inside. Never Cross a Witch with PMS.*" Isobel chuckled. "They remind me of our sleep shirts."

"The glamour-witch bookends were Mom's. The books were Aunt Fiona's."

"So, your mother was a witch, too?"

"Do you have a problem with that?"

"Heck no, that's the most refreshing thing I've heard about your family. The way Brandy tells it, you're all so utterly dysfunctional, like my family, I know, but the more I know you, the more fascinating you all seem."

"Yeah, well, stick around a while. I might lean toward the craft myself, though I keep pulling myself back. Mostly."

"I'm sticking." Isobel picked up the naughty witch

book. "Believe me; I'd like to see how that witchcraft thing turns out for you. Heck, I may join you."

We scarfed down our hip-widening brownies, each bite followed by caffeine- and sugar-shot chasers.

"Awesome," Isobel said, going limp in the chair. "I'm too heavy to get up, now, but too happy to care."

"That'll cost you a five-mile run tonight *and* tomorrow morning, but every once in a while you gotta go for the sin in sinsational."

"You call that sin?" Isobel asked.

"For me, it is, because I'll never fit in my clothes if I keep that up. Ever have a Dos Equis with margarita pie?"

"You're going to be good for me. My sister and cousin were too much into, well, let's say, scarier substances, the kind one runs to—or from."

I sat straight up on the fainting couch. "What are you talking about? Should you have told Werner about that?"

"I haven't been questioned yet."

I relaxed. "Oh, right. But you said 'were.' Has something happened to your twin that you haven't mentioned?"

"Not that I know of. I'll be honest with the detective when he comes to question me. Don't worry."

"That reminds me. Someone called here several times to find out if you'd arrived safely. He said he was your brother. Should you call him back?"

"I think not. I don't have a brother. Curious. Did he leave a number?"

"Isobel, you don't call the guy who makes a crank call and uses your first name."

"You didn't say he was a crank."

Or a murderer. "I must have misunderstood the call," I said, so she wouldn't be afraid. Definite threat in the caller's tone. Altered voice. No caller ID. Should someone tell Isobel she was in danger? I'd ask Werner. Alone. "So . . . your father is some kind of politician?"

"*Some* kind. Let's open the trunk."

I raised my cheering arm. "Yes!"

She knelt beside it, opened the envelope at the end of the yellow ribbon, and handed me the key.

I slipped it into the lock, my heart pumping triple time. "Vin-tage clothes, vin-tage clothes, vin-tage clothes!" I sang with each beat.

I caught her surprise. "Sorry, I'm like a cheerleader for my own life choice."

"Go, you. I wish I could be, though dress design, I suspect, just might do it for me."

"Your dad is running for selectman?" I asked as I lifted back the trunk's top. I opened a drawer in the shallow top tray and found insulin syringes, a dozen or so. "What's this?"

"Oh, Grand-mère's a diabetic. She probably forgot they were there."

I lifted that tray off the inside top and covered my mouth with clenched fists when in a lower, deeper bin, I saw three pairs of fifties high-top roller skates in pink, aqua, and yellow.

"I'll tell you about my dad's bid for office in a minute. Do you think that roller skating is as good as running? I mean to work off chocolate-frosted orgasms?"

I beamed. "Worth a try. Will they fit?"

"The best thing about Grand-mère is that we wear the same size shoes. My one great memory of Payton is us as preteens roller-skating in Grand-mère's ballroom. Right now, I'm going to skate in memory of the Payton I once loved."

Isobel and I were up on wheels in no time. "Good thing I got a high-impact finish on my floors. They said I'd be able to drive a Mack truck in here and not mar the finish."

"That *was* smart. Plus you left an empty space the size of a skating rink behind your check out counter and between your tea buffet and seating area. Let's put these wheels and your floor finish to the test. Here's to Payton!" she said, zipping off.

"To Payton!" Thinking on my wheels, I raised my sailor skirt halfway up my thighs, and I was off. "Oh, it's just like riding a bike," I said.

"And having sex," Isobel added. "The minute you get back on, you remember how."

I lost my concentration, ran into the fainting couch, and landed belly-first, skates on one side, head and arms on the other.

I felt especially graceful with Isobel splitting a gusset.

"Hey," I called. "Cut it out. I'm not sure the couch can stand a 'laughed so hard, I peed my pants' event."

Memorializing Isobel's cousin, tossed against my furniture like a rag doll, I still found my first morning with my intern to be so much better than I'd originally expected.

I pulled myself up and sat on the fainting couch to catch my breath. "Oh, and I was congratulating myself on making you laugh."

Isobel was now having a good noisy cry.

"Payton and I may have roller-skated together as kids, but she didn't grow up to be the same cousin I loved. Don't mind me; I'm crying for a friend I lost a long time ago."

I grabbed a couple of tissues off an old art deco side table, got on my skates, and handed them to Isobel—in passing as it turned out—because I kept going, despite my attempt at an effortless stop, and rolled right into the dressing room.

I hit a swinging door. "Ouch." I rubbed my nose. "One way or another, I'm afraid I'm gonna break my . . . shop," I said, emerging.

Isobel's emotion had turned on a dime. "I like you, boss."

"Right back at'cha, Isobel York. Now tell me what office your dad is running for, and let's glide in gentle circles around the open area, here, no wall-kissing or ass fractures."

Fifteen

The same costume will be Indecent ten years before its time, Shameless five years before its time, Outré (daring) one year before its time, Smart [in its own time], Dowdy one year after its time, Ridiculous twenty years after its time, Amusing thirty years after its time, Quaint fifty years after its time, Charming seventy years after its time, Romantic one-hundred years after its time, Beautiful one-hundred-and-fifty years after its time. —JAMES LAVER

Isobel saluted and roller-skated off, executing a graceful and perfect circle around the open area.

"You've done this before," I said.

"Hell yes. Grand-mère taught us to skate from an early age. One of us, at least, was supposed to win the Olympics. It was part of her plan for a life of keeping the Yorks in the limelight. Publicity is her middle name. None of her granddaughters went for it, though."

"May I ask, though you don't have to answer, where your mother was during your formative years?"

"My mother and her twin were a popular song and dance team who didn't need toddlers holding them back."

Popular? "Would I have heard of them?"

"Probably. The Yada-Yadas?"

"Your mother was one of the singing Spinyadas? I loved them. My father took me to see their cabaret show on Broadway for my sixteenth birthday. Their pacing was superb, their dancing routines unmatched, and the range of their voices blew me away."

"Everybody who didn't expect to be tucked in at night by their mothers loved them."

"I remember their televised double wedding." And the search when their plane went down. "Was your mother Muffy or Buffy? And were those stage names?"

"*Not* stage names."

Interesting bottom line: Quincy York, politico, son of a publicity-hungry matriarch, aka Grand-mère, and his brother, had married world-class celebrities.

"We were all three girls," Isobel continued, "raised by our respective nannies. Mostly, we grew up like three sisters, more a part of our two nannies' families than our own."

"While your mothers were touring the world performing, where were your fathers?"

"As much in the limelight as possible, one way or another. Payton's father is in prison now for embezzlement, on a humongous scale, while my father is finished running other people's campaigns and is currently running for first selectman of Kingston's Vineyard."

"Werner told me about his campaign, but I never heard of Kingston's Vineyard."

"Never, *ever* say that within hearing of a Kingston or a York."

"Did I offend you? I'm sorry."

Isobel chuckled. "No, your lack of knowledge tickles me, but I'm considered the black sheep of the family. Most people have never heard of Kingston's Vineyard. It's seven miles off the coast, at the point where Rhode Island meets Massachusetts, in perfect alignment with the state line.

"It's rather unique in that it's an island split, smack up the middle, by the two states. It's pretty much a private island, first owned and populated by the Kingstons, but it's governed by both states. Ninety per cent of Kingston's Vineyard is still owned by my family, mostly Grand-mère, who won't let anyone forget she was a Kingston by birth."

"I remember the search for your mother and Payton's mother, but I don't remember the outcome."

"It's been eleven years now, and I can't forget. Their private plane went down somewhere near the Hawaiian Islands. After a massive search, only a few small plane parts were ever found. My family waited the seven years and had my mother and her twin declared dead."

"How sad your life has been." I turned to roller-skate backward so I could face her. "I'm sorry."

"Don't feel bad," she said. "We hardly knew them. Motherly hugs were given in front of the cameras for publicity before tours."

Change of subject. "The way your dad's campaign manager treated him, you'd think he was running for governor or something."

"Lieutenant governor is the next step, next election, according to Grand-mère."

I stopped by the trunk and removed the second, deeper wooden bin from the top. "Hey, all these clothes have been dry-cleaned."

"Of course they have. Grand-mère would do nothing less."

I picked out a pretty aqua cap that matched the skates, the kind a fifties stewardess might once have worn, and I put it on. "Cute, hey?" I'd never gotten psychometric visions from a hat, though I supposed there was always a first time, but since the skates proved safe, I felt pretty secure wearing the hat. "Lieutenant governor of which state?" I asked. "Rhode Island or Massachusetts?"

"Either one would be acceptable, though Massachusetts *is* bigger. Grand-mère will take what she can get."

"What she can get for your father, that is."

"Sure. It's all for him. So not."

I chuckled. "I'm not the only one with snark."

"Thank you." She executed a skater's dip and popped back up again to twirl in the center of our wider circle. "Thank you very much," she said, her voice humming from her spin.

"Eve, my best friend, is gonna like you." Or hate her. I couldn't quite make up my mind how Eve would feel.

As for myself, I could easily become a good friend to Isobel York, though I *should* be her boss first.

"Hey, follow me," I said. "I want to get an empty rack from behind Paris When It Sizzles."

"Oh," Isobel said, roller-skating down the center of the sales floor after me, between nooks of clothes, taking in the merchandising section of the shop for the first time. "Love that the cubbies have fashionable addresses in retro street-name frames on vintage lampposts."

"The cubbies on the left were once horse-drawn hearse stalls, so when I remodeled, I had matching stalls built facing them."

"Excuse me? Did you say horse-drawn hearse stalls?"

"This building once belonged to the Underhill Funeral Chapel as a carriage house. Wait till you see what I have upstairs. The cubby walls on the right are movable. Later, I can put stalls where we skated or I can widen these. I could also raise the roof to make a second selling area one floor up."

"Why raise the roof?"

"Living quarters and work space. You saw my dad and Fiona last night. I think they deserve some privacy. But raising the roof is a project for the future. I also need to build a stairway to the cellar. I might be able to use that for storage or a work area with a bit of remodeling."

"How can you have no stairway to your cellar?"

"I didn't say we didn't have a way to get down there. There's a coffin elevator with access from upstairs.

Dumb construction crew covered it up on this floor in the dressing room, formerly the horse stalls."

Isobel clapped her hands. "Your sister Brandy didn't do your shop justice at all. I'd heard of you, of course. Who hasn't? But this place is spectacular. I love it here," Isobel said. "And look at this layout. You clever girl, not only are the streetlamps an inspiration but the names you gave the streets. Shoe Heaven, Bag Lady, Eternals, Little Black Dress Lane, Very Vintage, Unique Street, Around the World, Mad as a Hatter, and now I understand what you meant, Paris When It Sizzles."

I pulled an empty rack on wheels, full of clanging hangers, from behind Paris, and she grabbed the other end. "I toyed with naming the nooks after designers, but there are too many, and this way, I can mix it up and entice my customers into looking at everything."

On the way back, Isobel roller-skated while pulling the rack behind her, and I skated pushing it from the rear.

"Thank you, boss, for this opportunity to intern with you. I'll do a smashing job, I promise."

I had an unsettling feeling she would, except that working wouldn't be the end of our relationship.

I'd heard enough this morning about her family to make me fear that Payton did not die of natural causes, and I already cared too much about Isobel to ignore my inner sleuth any longer.

Sixteen

I love those bras that "enhance" shape, although (when all is said and done) they can be deceiving. But, by the time I have a girl's bra off, I'm so happy just to be there, I'm willing to live with the deception.

—RICH SANTOS, *MARIE CLAIRE* MAGAZINE

"Tell me about the family island," I suggested, going with my gut by gathering background information for the case. "Sounds fascinating. I'd like to visit it sometime."

"It's not so much fascinating as a bit freaky and greedy. I feel as if the Kingston-Yorks are on the take and out for anything they can get. The idea is to make Kingston's Vineyard bigger than Martha's Vineyard. Well, it already is in acreage but not in tourism. The mighty dollar and all that. Grand-mère sees my dad, sonny boy number one, the hands-down favorite son, as having the political potential of a Kennedy, and ain't nobody gonna get in his way."

"Who would stop them . . . if someone dared get in his way, I mean?"

"Grand-mère, the old dear; she'll stop them. Ruthless son of a—"

"Stitch?"

"Yeah, that."

"Except that she's a daughter not a son," I pointed out.

"That's her biggest regret, her sex, or *she'd* be in the White House. She's sure of it."

"Are you a mole for the opposition?"

Isobel snorted, but she turned beet red as we set the rack near the trunk. And I wondered why she should be so deeply embarrassed to go against the family's political aspirations.

I used an old roller-skating trophy to root around in the clothes, so I wouldn't touch anything, while Isobel lost her embarrassment. "Wanna hear a huge family secret?" she asked.

"Do kimonos have frog closures? Of course I want to know the family secret." I grabbed a hanger and slipped it into the sweetheart neck of a sleeveless, fifties full-skirted dress of sheer cotton organdy in off-white with red-flocked polka dots, a red cummerbund, and a thin red stripe about six inches from a hem that would have fallen to right below the knee. I hung it on the rack. I supposed I might have been okay touching the dry cleaner's plastic over it, but I didn't dare test my theory.

"Let's get this stuff on hangers while you talk," I suggested, not bothering to remove the skates, because frankly, I wanted to fly a bit more. And if no customers showed up on this sunny June day, maybe we'd skate around the building and enjoy my fresh tarmac parking lot.

Isobel hung a yellow sleeveless boatneck dress, trimmed with two four-inch bands of glittery gold and white-silk stitching and beadwork at the neck and around the center of the swing skirt.

"Okay, here's the story of the family secret. The original Kingston settled an uninhabited island when he got out of prison around 1828, *after* he kidnapped his bride—who he never married. Everybody on the mainland was so afraid of him, they left him alone for a generation, until after his thirty-two children were born—"

"Wait," I said, attaching a circle skirt printed with the New York skyline to a hanger, by touching only the skirt clips. "Thirty-two children with a woman he kidnapped? Did she not know how to row a boat for heaven's sakes?"

"Sorry, forgot to say he had two wives, one after the other, not at the same time. They each bore him sixteen children." Isobel hung a little black bubble dress with a gull-winged top, thin strapped, and self-belted. Probably Chanel.

"Okay, I'm not judging," I said, putting a banded wrap near its matching yellow sleeveless boatneck dress. "So two women bore him thirty-two children. Then what?"

"Payton's father used to tell a joke about that: At bedtime Convict Kingston used to ask his deaf wife, 'Do you wanna sleep, or what?' and she'd say, 'What?'"

"Payton's father's a chip off the old convict block, isn't he? He went to prison like his forefather."

Isobel covered her mouth with the palm of a hand for a minute. "I never thought of that. Poor Uncle Patrick. On the upside, his being true to the Kingston name might cheer Grand-mère."

"You have a weird family."

"You don't know the half of it."

God help me.

"Eventually, the thirty-two men and women started showing up on the mainland to look for husbands and wives of their own—who they *mostly* married—and all of it led to the mainlanders discovering the beauty of the island."

"At least the islanders didn't inbreed."

"I never thought of that. You know, that could account for a few anomalies."

I coughed for a bit before I caught my breath. "Whatever happened to the kidnapped 'bride'?"

"She died in childbirth."

"Yeah, well, the odds *were* in her favor."

"Yep, baby number sixteen killed her. So the handsome convict went to Newport, Rhode Island, and married him a rich young bride, because his island was discovered to be worth a fortune by then, as was he, especially after he sold a few lots to some of the Belleview Avenue mansion set, and the die was cast. Bottom line, his bride made him respectable and gave him sixteen more children. Bride number two outlived him by thirty years."

"Lucky her," I said. "At least she caught a break."

"With thirty-two kids to raise? I don't think so." Isobel hung a summer set, thin stripes of lime, pink, and turquoise, cut straight on the shorts with the same stripes cut on the bias on the angled top bearing only a single shoulder strap, and a contrasting turquoise slit-front skirt like the one Grace Kelly wore for the car-chase picnic in *To Catch a Thief.*

"Think of the fights wife two had to referee. We Kingstons, we fight all the time. Must be our convict blood."

That struck us both funny, and we laughed as if we'd OD'd on tequila shots rather than sugar and caffeine.

I remembered funerals where family members laughed more than usual, and I recognized it as a coping mechanism, so Isobel's loquaciousness and hilarity, especially today, didn't strike me as particularly odd. Besides, Brandy had characterized her as "outgoing," and that she was. "Pay dirt," I said. "Skating outfits!"

"Silly Mad. They're carhop outfits."

"Put the yellow one on to match your skates," I suggested.

She pointed to the stash. "There's the aqua one to match your hat and roller skates."

115

Did I dare try it on? "Oh, you look smashing in yours."

I unbuttoned my sailor dress and let it fall to the floor. Then I stepped gingerly out of it, careful not to roll into a split. "So, what does a first selectman do?" I asked, allowing her to release more of her pent-up emotions in any way she pleased, and if that fed my sleuthing instincts, so be it.

"According to my grandmother, any first selectman—especially my father—walks on water," Isobel explained while skating beautifully. "But on Kingston's Vineyard in particular, the first selectman is, foremost, the chairman of the board of selectmen. Historically, he's like a mayor on a smaller scale, with similar ceremonial duties. On the island, he's the town manager's boss, town CEO, and chief administrative officer. He's also a voting member of the board of selectmen and will often cast the tie-breaking vote for the finance and school boards, among others."

"So he runs the show?" I said, ready to slip my arms into the aqua miniskirted, button-front carhop outfit.

"Actually, he does what his mother tells him to, though it's really his campaign manager who does the dirty work. They've been friends since junior high. Ruben would lie, kill, steal, or die for my dad, but you didn't hear that from me."

"*I* heard it from you," Werner said. "Madeira . . ." He whistled his appreciation. "I'll never look at pineapple whip the same way again."

"Chauvinist." Twice in one day he sees my yellow bra. I closed the aqua outfit. "Have you been peeping *and* eavesdropping?"

He stole the last brownie from the box, took a huge bite, and made a sound that gave me the shivers. "Mm. Hailey's Pastries?"

"You're changing the subject, but yes."

"I wasn't really eavesdropping," he said, popping the last of *my* brownie into his mouth. "If you had looked up, you would have seen me come in. Ms. York, I nearly brought your father. Lock the door the next time you have a 'you didn't hear that from me' moment. And you both might want to lock up before you strip, though I don't mind in the least."

"Good advice," I said. "You owe me a brownie."

"I owe you a knot on the head, too, but you don't see me paying that back."

"Oh." I heard myself from a wobbly distance. "I'm gonna be sick."

Seventeen

The origins of clothing are not practical. They are mystical and erotic. The primitive man in the wolf-pelt was not keeping dry; he was saying: Look what I killed. Aren't I the best?
—KATHARINE HAMNETT

I think Werner scooped me into his arms, because the next minute he was setting me down in the bathroom. Then I was roller-skating across a field of tarmac, Patti Page singing "The Tennessee Waltz" in the background. I zigzagged past other carhops in aqua outfits, and of course, they were going to and from a parking lot of big-ascot, tail-finned cool cars.

I couldn't be Isobel or any of the cousins. None of us had been alive in that era. And why I was the wearer, rather than the casual observer, like on the boat, I didn't know. Maybe my placement in a vision had as much to do with the owner of the outfit. Single owner; I became that person. Multiple owners; I became an observer. Who knew? Was there such a thing as a guide to psychometric visions?

At any rate, I was most likely Grand-mère, herself, since these were her clothes, though this didn't seem like the job for a hotshot matriarch, à la Rose Kennedy.

The music piped into the lot sounded like a jukebox version of Bill Haley & His Comets' "Rock Around the Clock."

Nick and Werner would love the cars. I read each logo, models familiar to the real carhop of the past but not to Madeira Cutler: Nash, Packard, Studebaker, and a Pontiac Chieftain that could be the forerunner of the hatchback. New car names were Kaiser and Crosley Hotshot; the latter a convertible, two-seater.

"Yo, Lizzie," called a girl who stopped in front of me, and whose blouse had Pattie embroidered on it.

I looked down at my own blouse. Yep. Lizzie. I looked back at the drive-in. A diner quilted in silver and polished to a mirror shine: Rudy's Red Hots in flashing red and yellow neon up top. Probably famous for hot dogs, not teeny red candies.

"Got a guy in that salmon and black Chevrolet," Pattie said, "who wants to see you, specific like." She popped her bubble gum.

"Coming right up." On the way, I gave the guy in the Crosley Hotshot his check for a dollar thirty-two, then I let him count his nickels while I zoomed on over to the black and salmon number. Barf. Ugliest colors I ever saw on a car.

Mitch Miller belted out an enthusiastic round of "The Yellow Rose of Texas," and both of me loved it.

"Hey, good lookin'," the driver said, slicking back his DA.

"What can I do you for?" I asked.

"The name's Perry," said the Jimmy Dean type. "Seven o'clock, Four Square Motel on the pike. Here's your tip, and I'll have fries with my catsup."

"Sure thing." I saluted and zoomed away, glanced at my tip and . . . hel-lo—

I ran smack into a frumpy black Mercury coupe and didn't know what surprised me more: the bruise on my leg, the ticked nun behind the wheel, or Perry's tip: a brass motel key wrapped in a hundred dollar bill.

Still, I got a wash of Liz's satisfaction in providing for a young family. Her husband, the bum, spent his time at the Dew Drop Inn or playing the ponies. Never home. Never a paycheck.

He knew nothing about this money she earned, but she kept her boys fed and invested for the future.

She was a good mom.

I couldn't fault her for her cause.

Somebody slapped me. I thought it was the nun.

"Ouch. That hurts. Werner? What are you, some kind of Neanderthal? I never took you for the brutal type."

"Are you all right?" he asked, a little pale.

"I feel a lot better," I said. "Thought I was gonna be sick. Guess not."

"Guess again. Damn straight you were sick. As a dog. That was me holding your hair back and cleaning you up, except that you were out cold." He ran a shaking hand through his hair while in his other he held a damp washcloth to the back of my neck.

Isobel rolled into the doorway. "You okay, boss?"

"I am now. Guess I wasn't for a while."

"If you call humming fifties tunes with your eyes closed and calling Werner, Sister, I guess you weren't. You were a little bit funny," she admitted. "What group sang 'Earth Angel'?"

"The Penguins," Werner and I answered together.

He shook his head, rinsed the cloth, and wiped my brow, my neck, and down toward my cleavage.

"Hey, my uniform's unbuttoned."

He dropped the cloth and went to work on that. "I'm *buttoning* it, now that you're not such an armful. Not my fault you passed out half-dressed."

Someone growled, and Werner and I both looked up.

"Nick? You okay?"

He growled louder and pointed to the lower half of his face. "Wired shut!" he had already printed on the notebook he pulled from his navy T-shirt pocket.

"I'm so sorry," I groaned while Werner finished buttoning my uniform, and that's when I looked down at his hands and noticed my name tag.

"Isobel," I called as I exited the bathroom before the injured men in my life. "What was your grandmother's name?"

"Elizabeth, but you can call her Beth, Betsy, Betty, Lizbeth, Eliza, Lizzie. Why?" Isobel continued roller-skating.

Bette? "I just wondered." . . . how she would sound through a voice modulator.

Lizzie? I'd just carhopped in Lizzie's roller skates. "Isobel, does your grandmother travel in a chauffeured powder blue stretch limo?"

Isobel stopped dead. "Oh, no. Has she been checking up on me again?"

"She has if Bette is an alias."

"That's her. Making sure I don't screw up her plans and shame the family."

I shook my head, gave Nick a meaningful look, and smoothed my bodice. "This carhop outfit I'm wearing used to belong to Isobel's grandmother. I believe she was a carhop in her youth, right, Isobel?"

"Absolutely, at three different diners, actually."

I'd learned from that vision that Grand-mère was self-made, and one man had given her a key wrapped in money. It didn't seem connected to the first vision at all, but then, most early visions seemed disconnected.

Understanding lit Nick's expression. He *knew* I zoned when I got a reading on a vintage outfit. Werner, however, did not know about my psychic gifts, and he never would.

Nick had kept my secrets since we were kids, even the weird ones, like psychometry later in life. As for Werner, well, him mocking me by calling me glamazon in third grade, which inspired my "Little Wiener" comment, sort of put him out of the running for secret keeper.

After Eve, Nick had been my second-main confidant, many times in a romantic way. Now, as a friend.

Werner was, and always had been, as he put it, my frenemy. As in "keep your frenemies close." And I was certainly doing that today; yellow lace, front hook, push-up bra *close*.

But these days, Werner and I were mostly leaving our polite, if distant, frenemy relationship behind, eerily rising above it toward a "What a messy, seam-ripping clustertuck this is. And give me the pinking shears so I can slit my throat, in a bloody jagged-edged sort of way."

I looked at the two men in my life, sizing each other up, and thought, Why me?

"Miss York," Werner said, addressing Isobel. "I need to ask you a few questions about your cousin's death, if you don't mind."

"Should I take off my skates?"

Werner winced. "As long as you leave your dress on, I don't care."

Nick grunted.

I made us a pot of tea, just to have something to do. Nice, tummy-soothing chamomile tea.

Isobel agreed to be questioned by Werner in the empty dressing room area so they could have some privacy.

"Cupcake?" Dolly Sweet called from the front door. "Are you here?"

"I have to get the bell back up on that door," I said to no one in particular. "I can't take all these surprise customers."

The Sweets dropped in every Sunday like clockwork after twelve o'clock Mass. Personally, I think Dolly would have stopped going to church long ago if the shop wasn't calling her name.

I knew what she wanted from her visits to Vintage Magic. She wanted, well, magic. She strutted on by me as I went to greet her and Ethel, and she went right to Paris When It Sizzles "to look for a new shawl," she told her daughter-in-law.

Ethel had no idea that her wild mother-in-law had never mended her wayward ways and was still having assignations with her old lover, Dante Underhill, ghost. For some reason Dolly, Fiona, and I were the only people who could see Dante, but I could never figure out why the giggles coming from Paris sizzling didn't make an impression on Ethel, unless Dolly knew Ethel was too deaf to hear.

Nick winked at me.

"It kills me that you can't talk," I said, "and it's all my fault. Want me to kiss it better?" After all, I had kissed Werner better. What was wrong with me?

Nick raised both hands to ward me off.

"Too mad at me or too sore?"

He opened both hands, like a mime who's blameless, then he curled a finger in a come-hither way.

Werner came out of the dressing room, walked rudely between us—uber symbolic—raised my chin with a curl of his finger, then pointed his thumb over his shoulder at Nick. "That guy's got a chip on his shoulder the size of Mount Rushmore carved in *your* likeness."

Werner looked straight at me. "You pack a wallop, kiddo, in so many ways."

He went straight out the door, having demonstrated his lack of fear in poking the tiger.

And from the moment he chucked me under the chin to when I realized I was staring at a closed door, I felt . . . special.

I turned away and caught Nick's disapproval.

"You and I are off again, remember? Friends."

Ethel's head came up. "You and Nick are off? Is that true, Nick?"

"He can't talk," I said. "His mouth's wired shut. I broke his jaw last night."

Eighteen

And by my grave you'd pray to have me back
So I could see how well you look in black.
—MARCO CARSON

I couldn't have Nick and Werner both. But since Nick was no longer my boy toy, literally, I wanted them *both* as friends.

Was that weird?

"Sorry, Nick. I guess I shouldn't have admitted I broke your jaw. Ethel, Nick walked into Fiona's dark house when I was freaked by threats to my new intern; she was with me. So I attempted to protect her."

Nick rolled his eyes.

"Where is your new intern, cupcake?"

"Isobel's in the dressing room, I think. She'll be out in a minute, and I'll introduce her to you and Dolly. Nick, I'm not powerful enough to have made a strike to your ego. For the love of Hermès, you're FBI Special

Agent Nick Jaconetti. You fight copperheads in the deadly swamps of . . . wherever copperheads . . . copper."

Nick raised a brow.

"Well, you don't see Werner sending me black looks."

Ethel giggled. "That's because the handsome-as-sin Detective Werner's got his eye on you."

"Really? I hadn't noticed."

"What didn't you notice?" Ethel asked. "How handsome he is? Or that he's carrying a torch for you?"

"Yeah, that." I put all my attention into shaping the turquoise ribbon on the tea roses in the yellow Lucite purse with the broken lid on my counter.

Setting vases of flowers in battered handbags calmed my angst over ill-treated purses and puppy-eyed exes.

Dolly made her saucy way back up the aisle toward us between vintage nooks, holding Dante's arm, looking a little weird, I'm sure, to anybody who couldn't see the hunky ghost. She cackled as only Dolly could, as if she read my mind. "You did too know about Werner's interest in you, Madeira Cutler. Everybody in town knows."

"Fuzzy pink elephant slippers! Tell me it isn't so. Wait. I'll bet my father doesn't know."

"He'd be the only one," Dolly said, "but that would be typical of him, since he doesn't know he loves poor Fiona."

Isobel came out of the dressing room sometime after

Werner left and skated her slow way to the counter, her eyes puffy.

I pretended not to notice, so as not to embarrass her, as I introduced her to the Sweets.

Seeing Nick seemed to cheer her up.

Really? Just because I didn't want him didn't mean I wanted anybody else to have him.

"Sorry your jaw's broken," she said, shaking his hand. "If it's any consolation, you look a lot better now than you did last night and this morning."

The Sweets' radar went up so fast, multiple antennae about poked me in the eye.

Isobel had been gathering her emotions together after talking to Werner, but she might also have been listening to us and learning the lay of the land. Meanwhile, the Sweets thought she spent the night with Nick.

To correct or not correct . . .

Aw, let the gossips have some fun. Correcting them will give Nick something to concentrate on when he can talk again, and it'll boost his bruised ego for his Mystick Falls neighbors to think the young Isobel was interested in him—and in the process they'll discover that he and I broke up.

"Isobel gave me a trunk of her grandmother's clothes from the fifties," I told the Sweets. "Ethel, would you like to help us put them on hangers?"

At Vintage Magic, Ethel loved to help.

Dolly loved to canoodle. Her word.

"You know how much I love to help, cupcake." Ethel said. She took Isobel's arm. "Don't be sad to leave your family, dear. Vintage Magic is a wonderful shop, and Madeira's a sweetie. We helped raise her, you know."

It was true. The whole town helped after my mother died, Aunt Fiona and the Sweets more than anyone. Before school plays, the Sweets knew the lines better than we kids. And how many sports events can two elderly ladies actually *want* to attend? Didn't matter. They attended them all. Bar none. Winter and summer.

Sometimes I thought maybe the Cutlers gave the Sweets a reason to go on, kept them young and all.

Dolly shrugged. "I can't decide between Paris When It Sizzles and some good old fifties clothes."

"Hey," Dante said. "You wanna remember the fifties or relive them?" He wiggled his brows, and she let him take her back *to* Paris . . . and the fifties.

That nook never sizzled the way it did when they used it.

Dante's new energy and his ability to move things, like opening and closing doors, might make him more fun, which Dolly would certainly appreciate.

My cell phone rang, and though I didn't recognize the number, I picked it up because of all the prep going on for Brandy's fund-raiser this Saturday and Sherry's baby shower on Sunday.

"The tents?" I asked. "Yes, of course, I still need them. You still have the deposit, don't you? No, I don't want my money back. I want the bleeping tents! What? You can't cancel on me three days before a nationally advertised fund-raising event."

I listened to the guy's excuses with half an ear. "I don't care if you have to rent them yourself from the wilds of Africa and have them caravanned in by elephant train, I want those tents delivered, as contracted, to the Vancortland estate this coming Friday before eight A.M., or you'll hear from my lawyer, my sister's lawyer, the Nurture Kids Foundation lawyer, the Vancortland lawyer—"

"Good idea. You do that."

I clapped my phone shut. "Amazing how the word 'lawyer' clears everything up."

Nineteen

The erogenous zone is always shifting, and it is the business of fashion to pursue it, without ever catching it up.

—JAMES LAVER

"What was that about?" Isobel asked, though it was obvious everyone wanted to know.

"Oh, Brandy's fund-raising event. The Carousel of Love fund-raiser next weekend on the Vancortland estate grounds. We need the tents in case of rain, though I'd rather see them used for keeping the attendees and donors out of the sun and to serve up some iced refreshments."

"When is Brandy coming home?" Dolly asked. "Isn't she cutting it a bit close?"

Ethel elbowed her mother-in-law. "How well do we know Brandy?"

Dolly chuckled. "Right," she said. "She often cuts things close, but how could she plan such a big event from the Peace Corps?"

I raised a brow.

"Of course," Ethel said. "You planned it."

"To be fair, Brandy's not with the Peace Corps, any-more. She's with the Nurture Kids Foundation, and she was able to send invites to their connections and some of her own donor friends from New York, where she cur-rently lives and works for the foundation. From here, I invited my vintage clothing collector friends, like Mel-ody Seabright and Kira Fitzgerald Goddard, who came to my last fashion show. And they invited their friends, the Cartwright sisters, all four, because they have their own vintage clothing shop, the Immortal Classic. I also let all of my shop customers and Cort's vintage car en-thusiast buddies know about the event."

All the time I was talking, Nick ran a finger up and down my spine, a sensation I adored, and he knew it. His silent seduction didn't last long, because I shivered, and Dolly silently chided him.

Nick reclaimed his hand.

"Brandy will be here after six tonight," I said, ignor-ing their looks. "And she'll run with the rest of the prep." No need to be catty and tell the truth, that she'd still probably leave it to me.

"What does she have left to do when she gets here, for the event, I mean?" Isobel asked, hanging another carhop minidress, this one hot pink with a black poodle on the skirt.

My mind worked in one direction while I answered in

another. "She has to call the VIP invitees, personally, to remind them about the importance of the weekend. Everything else is done—from getting Cort's vintage auto club buddies to bring their cars, to the fifties clothes for the models who'll show off each car like they did in the fifties, matching them for style and looking pretty. OMG," I said. "Let's put three of them in carhop outfits. How utterly pulled-together that would look, though I didn't know we'd have carhop outfits at our disposal."

Nick put his arm around my neck and pulled me back against him. I turned in his embrace, wrapped my arms around his waist, and laid my head on his chest. "Thanks for the sign of approval. I'm so very sorry I hurt you."

He pulled me around the corner between the counter and the door, grabbed a notebook, and wrote, "Sorry I didn't trust you."

"That kiss dream happened months ago, but I'll forgive you if you forgive me for beating the scrap out of you last night?"

"Done," he wrote.

"On again?" he printed, looking hopeful.

I sighed. "Friends, remember? There's too much I want to do with the shop. Faline ran the show in New York. The shop's my chance to do it my way. Little hint, though: I like to be appreciated. Not pampered or catered to, but not forgotten for months on end, either. And I'm not talking about your job but your attitude. Think about it."

"I will," he noted on his pad. "Werner appreciates you, doesn't he?"

"He does. I'll bring you some hot homemade broth to sip through a straw later, after I pick up Brandy at the train station, 'kay?"

His eyes twinkled, though he couldn't smile.

"We'll *talk*," I said.

He frowned.

"Sorry, bad joke. Just don't go getting any ideas."

He wrote, *"Moi?"* on the paper, touched his lips, then mine, and left.

I watched him cross the parking lot. The silent hunky type practiced in turning my knees to jelly. "You should get some rest," I yelled after him, and he raised his arm, his thumb and forefinger forming an O for "Okay."

When I got back to my worker bees hanging clothes from the trunk, so much more of Elizabeth Kingston York's clothing had been unpacked. Ethel may not have Dolly's sparkling personality or adventurous, try-anything attitude, but that woman could outwork a Fembot on speed.

"Is that a mink coat?" The animal lover in me fought with the fashionista. I read the label on the marvel of matched pelts. "Isobel, you're giving me a 1952 Christian Dior full-length mink coat?" I reached for it with both hands.

"Do not!" Eve shouted. "Touch that coat!"

I whisked my hands away and held them behind my back. "When did you get here?"

"Just this minute, thank the stars. I must be psychic. Oh, crap, no."

Isobel frowned. "Why can't she touch it?"

Eve's eyes widened. "She's . . . allergic . . . to mink. She found out at a . . . fashion show . . . in New York . . . I was there." Eve tilted her head, her expression focusing on me, her eyes conveying something like, "Help me, you time-traveling freak."

I had made peace with my psychometric gift. Eve had not.

Yes, I knew her well, though her fashion look of the week surprised me. She'd had her hair cut into a perfect pageboy *with* bangs, dyed white, with a blue streak braided near her face on one side. The braid was tied with a cluster of bright feathers and beads.

"Like the do?" she asked. "Kyle dared me."

"Kyle is good for you. I love the blue streak, the bright beads and feathers. You're actually wearing colors instead of all black. But really, did you have to euthanize a goldfinch, a cardinal, and maybe a hummingbird for that bouquet of feathers?"

"First of all, my new gothic steampunk look isn't all black. I wear earth tones now, mostly black and tan, it's true, with gold, brass, copper, and silver gears and stuff. The feathers and beads, they're man-made and come from a craft store. So, no dead birds, she who adores the hides of ittle bittie minks, leopards, bunnies, gators, and—"

"Snakes!" I added, and Eve shuddered, because she

hated snakes above all things. She especially detested their skin on a pair of shoes.

"I adore your look," Isobel said, like Eve was Madonna or Victoria Beckham, or *someone* whose ring she should kiss.

"Eve, this is Isobel York, my new intern, and Isobel, this is Eve Meyers, my best friend in the world. She saved my life when we were six."

"How'd a six-year-old do that?"

"Like an idiot, but that's beside the point," Eve said. "Mad, here, jumped off a big-ass whaleboat to retrieve the purse that matched her skirt. Dumb, hey? And Dumber, here, I jumped in after her to save her."

I put an arm around Eve. "We've been best pals ever since."

"How long ago was that?" Isobel asked.

"Nearly fifteen years ago," Eve said with a straight face, but Ethel's involuntary laugh gave us away. It was a rare day in hell that anybody could make Ethel laugh.

"We're a little bit older than you, Isobel," Eve said. "But we don't like to admit it."

"Hah!" Dolly said, joining us, Dante watching from his favorite chair. "I'm going on a hundred and four, and I'm proud of it."

"Yeah, well, the scales tip after a while," I said. "What else do we have in this bottomless trunk?"

"You, sit," Eve told me. "I'll help put the clothes on

hangers. I saw Werner. He said you were sick as a dog this morning."

"And you passed out at home." Isobel gasped. "Are you pregnant?"

I knelt and braced myself on the edge of the trunk. "Yeah, another one of those miracle conceptions, this time with the daughter of a witch. Wouldn't my mother be proud?"

The shop phone jarred us out of our amusement, its ring harsher than my cell phone, and Isobel raised a hand to stop me, as if answering was her job now. "Vintage Magic, Isobel York here. Can I—" She frowned, waited, paled, and hung up.

I knew that her picking up was a bad idea. "Did he speak with a scary voice from the tomb, like he wanted to chew you up and spit you out?"

"Yes to the voice, but his words were worse." She rubbed her arms and then crossed them tight in front of her. "He said, 'You're supposed to be dead.'"

Twenty

I wore a lot of vintage clothing. I dressed like a reporter, with
a little card in my hat. I had these fantasies of who I wanted
to be, so I'd dress like an explorer, a cowboy. I dressed up like
Elton John a lot too. That was another period.

—ILLEANA DOUGLAS

"We raised that girl better than this," I told my dad, as
we stood waiting for the six thirty train that night, trying
to figure out where we went wrong.

Sure, I'd been late because my phone was being
bugged by the police, but it didn't matter. It didn't look
like Brandy had made this train, either.

"This is my third trip to pick her up, and I swear if my
cell phone rings one more time while I'm standing on
this platform—"

"There she is," he said.

"Oh yeah, the one who looks like a refugee from a
thrift store Dumpster."

"Watch your tone, young lady," my father said. "Try
not to pick a fight on the first day."

"Sorry, Dad." Brandy was actually dressed better than Payton had been, and I thanked heaven Brandy came strutting up to us alive and safe and with a twinkle in her eyes. The twit, she'd dressed like that to yank my chain.

I chuckled, because suddenly her clothes didn't matter. She and her smile did.

Brandy threw herself into my father's arms, and I saw the glint of moisture in his eyes. He was such a great dad. While Sherry and I favored his side of the family, except that I had Mom's hair, if Brandy resembled anyone, even the slightest, it was Mom. In looks not demeanor, although she did have my mom's famous pure, stubborn determination. Now, our brother, Alex, he was a true mix of both parents, almost dad's clone in build and height, he was a man who fought, physically if necessary, for what he believed in, unlike a certain soft-spoken professor we loved. After all, an FBI agent would have to be a fighter.

Alex! Damn. Now that Nick, his partner, was out of commission, my brother would be pulled back to work to carry the load for them both. My sister-in-law, Tricia, was going to kill me when she heard *I* beat the scrap out of Nick. Though this early in her second pregnancy, she probably didn't pack as much of a wallop. I took comfort in that.

The whole family would be together this weekend for the fund-raiser. That would be great. I hugged my sister

Brandy and remembered how scared I'd been when I saw that ambulance yesterday. "Brandy, I'm so glad you're home safe."

"Safe? Do you think the world is any safer here in Mystic, just because this is a small town in a First World country? Do you think your high-fashion customers have never committed a crime? What about ignoring the hungry around the world?"

Ignore the dig. Ignore the dig. "My *high-fashion* customers make up two-thirds of your invitation list for this weekend. And they're generous to a fault, so lay off."

"I'm just saying." Her words indicated that she'd backed down but, woolly knobby knits, could that girl raise her nose any higher in the air?

I looked at my father, who shrugged and gave me the puppy dog look that begged me to keep the peace.

"Is Isobel here?" Brandy asked.

"Yes, and she's suggested we take you for a development director's makeover."

"I don't have time for a makeover," she said, throwing her torn duffel into the back of my Element like it was Nick's battered, secondhand, military-issue Hummer.

"Brandy, you don't have to go high-fashion, in fact you shouldn't," I said. "You want to look professional but not like you're wasting the foundation's money. Nevertheless, a development director should always represent a winning cause—"

"Five minutes, and you're going to tell me how to do my job and read me my faults? Besides, Nurture Kids isn't a winning cause. The foundation's in trouble, and donors need to know that."

"No, they don't. Giving to a losing cause is the same as flushing your money down a toilet. Focus on the foundation's positives. The good you do. The kids you've helped. And for heaven's sake, look successful."

"Dad, she's always telling me what to do. People are coming to help Nurture Kids, not to see what their development director is wearing."

"You know," my father said, with a familiar gleam. "This reminds me of a quote by Albert Einstein." He hugged us both, one on either side of him. "When Einstein's wife asked him to change clothes to meet the German ambassador, Einstein said, 'If they want to see me, here I am. If they want to see my clothes, open my closet and show them my suits.'"

I crossed my arms. "I'll bet Einstein wasn't wearing mismatched moccasins and a stained top."

My father squeezed my shoulder in retaliation for the comment and as a signal for me to cool it.

"The moccasins match; it's just that one of them was a window display and the other stayed boxed, so one is faded." Brandy chuckled. "Okay . . ." She looked down at herself as if getting it. "I agree to look as professional as I can afford to on a tight budget. Will you help me, Mad?"

I thought I might cry. "If you'll accept at least a weekend's worth of outfits as a gift, you're welcome to come to my shop and look around. I've got some classic business suits on sale simply because they're not as vintage as I'd like or by significant designers. And I know you're not into spikes, but think about comfy squash-heeled dress shoes or flats. I can probably set you up with a go-anywhere, mix-and-match wardrobe well-suited to a development director."

"Is tomorrow too soon?" Brandy asked. "I want to accept Cort's invitation to stay with him until Saturday, but I'd like to look good when I get to his place, though I didn't quite realize that until you pointed out my wardrobe's shortcomings."

"You're not staying at home while you're here?" my dad asked, looking only half-disappointed.

She chuckled, because we could all read him dreadfully well. "You don't mind, do you, Daddy?"

I rolled my eyes at her behind his back.

"'The father of a daughter is nothing but a high-class hostage,'" he quoted. "'A father turns a stony face to his sons, berates them, shakes his antlers, paws the ground, snorts, runs them off into the underbrush, but when his daughter puts her arm over his shoulder and says, "Daddy, I need to ask you something," he is a pat of butter in a hot frying pan.' That Garrison Keillor must have had at least *three* daughters."

We each kissed his cheek. "Hey, a dad sandwich."

"I like Cort," Brandy said, stepping back. "I'm flattered at the invite, and it'll be so much easier getting ready for the weekend if I make my fund-raiser's location home base. Supplies will be delivered for the next few days, after all. I can't believe you got Scotland's famous MacKenzie Carousel to stop at Cort's on its traveling exhibit across the U.S."

"Well, you can thank Melody Seabright and Kira Fitzgerald Goddard for that. Your cause is close to their hearts, and their best friend is Victoria Cartwright MacKenzie, wife of the MacKenzie Carousel owner, Rory MacKenzie, who is the great-great-great-grandson of the original carver."

"Point them out to me this weekend, will you, so I can thank them."

"I will, because that carousel has elevated your Carousel of Love garden party, vintage car show, and hunk auction, to fantasmagloriously unique. Plus I've got models in fifties dress to complement the cars, like in the fifties when they revealed a year's new line. The models'll walk around cars indicating their features, and they'll have the cars' stats to answer questions. With convertibles, the model will sit up on the back like in a fifties parade. Ticket sales are booming."

"You don't mind if I stay with Cort, do you, Mad?"

"I think it's a splendid idea, Sis." Yay.

"Dad," Brandy cajoled. "You know Mad and I will get along better if we don't live in the same house."

"You win," my father said. "But you're not going to Cort's tonight?"

"I'm bushed from fighting off a King Kong type who wanted me to move my paperwork so he could sit beside me in an otherwise empty train car."

"What do you mean, a King Kong type?" I asked, my sleuthing radar going up.

"First he steps into the train car like I'm the one he's looking for, then he zooms in like I'm carrying international secrets."

"What did he look like?"

"A Neanderthal. Wide shoulders, beefy hands, hairy knuckles, heavy beard. A thug. Made me nervous, I'll tell you, though I think the conductor read my body language, because he came through often enough."

All I could think about were the phone calls as I backed out of the train station parking lot, but I didn't expect one could use a voice modulator on the run. Even if it was the same person, how would he know Brandy could lead him to Isobel? "Did he get off here in Mystic?" If so, I needed to call Werner.

"I have no idea."

"I'm taking you both home," I told Brandy and my dad, "then I'm going to see Werner about the train thing. Dad, you and Isobel can fill Brandy in on what's been happening the past two days." I could have just called Werner, but I wanted to see if he had other information on the case, and I knew I had a better shot in person.

"Will do," my father said.

"Is Isobel staying at our house?" Brandy asked.

"Yes, she's resting right now. We didn't get a lot of sleep last night," I said, an understatement and a half.

I dropped them at my dad's house and didn't get out of the car. As soon as Aunt Fiona opened the front door and hugged Brandy, I pulled away.

I wondered if the hairy-knuckled Neanderthal and Isobel's threatening caller were one and the same person. My eyes welled up at the thought of either of them being that close to my sister. Though just because my caller sounded like a Neanderthal didn't mean it wasn't a blue-haired granny.

I made a stop for hot, clear broth at the nearest deli and drove over to Nick's.

I found him in bed. "Wow," I said, hands on my hips. "Nothing subtle about you."

He opened his arms.

I placed a quart of hot soup in one of his hands.

He jumped from the bed, set it on the nightstand, and gave me a frown.

I handed him a straw. "Now, sip."

In a pair of navy boxers, chest bare, he sat in his leather reading chair and did as he was told.

I threw an afghan over him, paced, and told him about the techno caller and the guy who accosted Brandy on the final leg of her train trip. I told him about the day she was *supposed* to leave and the caller who said she needed to re-sign her termination papers for the Peace Corps. How her backpack got snatched on that wild goose chase, causing a coincidental loss of her ticket. Linked to Isobel's ID going missing, I told him about Payton's death on the train Brandy missed, and Payton having Isobel's ID. And I told him about my psychometric visions on the boat and as a carhop. It was so nice to be able to share that. "Am I wrong to be nervous?"

He had long since stopped sipping his soup and now sat straight up.

He pulled a notepad over and scratched something on it: "Why tell me?"

"Because you're my go-to guy."

He scribbled a reply. "Hold that thought. Now go tell Werner what you told me, except for the visions." He used one of his hands to form a gun and mimed shooting himself in the head.

I kissed him on the brow, lost my breath at the way he looked at me—hunger and something more in his expression. The way my father looked at Fiona. Oy.

Again, why me?

He held out the notebook so I could read what he added in caps: "LISTEN TO YOUR GO-TO GUY."

Twenty-one

I never cared for fashion much, amusing little seams and witty little pleats: it was the girls I liked.   —DAVID BAILEY

Two more quick stops, then I took the direct route to the police station.

I hovered in Werner's doorway, and he looked up from his work. "Oh no," he said.

"You want me to leave?" I turned to go on my saucy red Louboutin follow-me heels.

"Wait. Have you come to strip for me again?" He looked me up and down. "Please say yes."

"Perv." I'd changed into Grand-mère's fifties white with red polka dots and cummerbund. I half expected it to give me a psychometric reading, but I guess it just didn't have anything to say; not this particular piece, anyway.

For Werner's benefit, I twirled so the dress would

flare, one of my favorite moves in a gathered skirt since I could walk. "It's from the fifties; I wore it in honor of our mutual love for fifties music."

He chuckled. "Until today, I didn't know we shared a mutual love for fifties music. It's not something I usually admit."

"I love the decade, which is why I talked Brandy into making her upcoming fund-raiser a fifties event. Pure luck or karma brought that trunk to my door in the middle of fitting everyone for the do."

"I thought Isobel brought that trunk to your door."

"Essentially, she did."

Werner ran a hand through his hair. "It makes me nervous to think that karma might have had anything to do with you falling half-naked into my arms this morning."

"I'd be nervous about it, too," I admitted, "if karma had anything to do with, well, us."

"So you understand my reaction? You've assaulted me in every way possible—including my senses—at one time or another. If karma had anything to do with it, I'd have to start wearing armor." He rubbed at his five o'clock shadow. "Just saying it out loud is like tempting fate."

I shrugged and tried to keep my mouth shut, though my mind raced as I thought of the ways fate *had* thrown us together, and just to scare him, I allowed him to see the twinkle in my eyes.

"You feel okay?" he asked. "Not nauseous or anything?"

"I'm not planning to barf on you, if that's what you mean. But thank you for holding my hair back this morning. Not that I remember."

"Blocking it myself, thanks."

See, when I passed out, I took this trip to the nineteen-fifties. Yeah, he'd buy that. "Too much chocolate," I said.

"I'm a detective; I knew that right away."

I hiccupped an involuntary chuckle as I opened my grocery bag and set a bottle of Dos Equis in front of him.

"You already sound drunk," he said. "Close my door." He had an eye twinkle of his own that I'd come to appreciate, one I often tried to elicit.

I closed his door, then I set down the six-pack and took one of our favorite Mexican beers for myself.

"Your tummy okay?" he asked. "You sure you're up to this?"

"Watch me and find out. So, do we have cause of death yet?"

"No, we don't. I probably never told you, but in ninety-five percent of deaths, the autopsy will reveal cause of death on the same day."

"And the other five percent?" I asked, confused.

"The only time you have to wait weeks for a cause of death is with a toxicology report tied to drug use."

"Your forensics lab found drugs?"

"It looks like she's a recreational user, an experimenter. Plus the medical examiner did find one fresh needle mark, but it didn't lead to anything definitive."

"You know, Isobel implied that her sister and cousin got into trouble, and it made me assume drug use."

"You know what assumptions are worth."

"I know," I said. "How about time of death? Do we know when she died?"

"She had to have died on that bench while the ambulance was on its way to her. The tip came from an anonymous 911 call. We're thinking a disembarking passenger saw her on the bench."

"So this isn't an FBI case? Though Nick's case is somehow entangled."

"Yes. No. Maybe. He's looking at some of the same players, big embezzlement case. Repeat that to Nick, and I'm toast. But this case is all ours. I mean, all mine."

I hid my satisfaction, but in my heart I did a happy dance. He was beginning to accept my sleuthing. He hadn't once said, "I can't discuss the case," or "Madeira Cutler, are you sleuthing again?"

I cleared my throat. "Next step, then?"

"The deceased will be on her way to the nearest forensics lab in the morning."

As Nick suggested, I told Werner about Isobel's deep-voiced caller saying she should be dead. I also told him about Brandy's train car gorilla.

Werner took notes as quickly as I could talk, though I

noticed that he didn't turn on his recorder the way he had with Isobel's father earlier.

"You're good at that. Can you read what you wrote?" I turned his notebook my way.

He turned it back his way. "I can read it, but I'm the only one who can."

"The only one who's allowed?"

He kept an end table–sized fireproof floor safe behind his desk—a stack of crime and investigative technique books on top. He reached over and swung the door open.

Inside, stacked, bound notebooks were topped by index cards with years, months, and case names.

"Ever heard of a database?" I asked. "Eve could set you up with a beauty."

"Got one, thanks. But I like to have a personal relationship with my cases. Notes remind me of an interviewee's facial expressions, the way some women cross their legs to distract you when they're lying."

I admired the wool gabardine out of him for his distinctive techniques. "It looks like those notepads only date back to January. Where does your secret decoder ring stash go from here?"

"That's classified, and you don't have a ring."

I raised my Dos Equis, and we clicked bottles.

"Here's to suspects," he said.

I raised my chin and looked him in the eye. "Got any?"

He tapped his notebook on his desk a couple times. "Definitely a few suspicious characters."

I batted my lashes. "I have a list, too."

"So we each have a list." The detective sipped his beer, his bright gaze boring into mine over the mouth of the bottle.

He swallowed and raised his chin. "Show me yours, I'll show you mine."

Twenty-two

Where's the man could ease a heart like a satin gown?
—DOROTHY PARKER

"I'm up for another bottle while I tell you about Isobel's freaky family. You?"

He nodded. "Every family is freaky. Even yours."

"Oh, especially mine. You don't know the half of it. My mother was a witch."

"Hah!" he said. "Mine still is."

We sipped our beer contemplatively for a minute, and I decided this wasn't the time to tell Werner I wasn't kidding about my mother, but I did recount what I'd learned about Isobel's unusual family.

Werner stopped writing and looked up as I opened another beer. "Then what?

"Then you showed up to keep me from puking into a trunk of primo vintage and killing a Dior mink."

"Right." He winced. "Tryin' to forget that." He sat back and steepled his fingers. "I'm not sure about the campaign manager," Werner said. "I don't trust a guy with so much clout, especially when it's somebody else's power. I'm waiting for his financials."

"Ruben Rickard. Isobel described him as her father's cutthroat protector," I said. "He's on my suspect list, too. I'll see if I can learn anything more about him."

"Who else is on your list?" Werner asked.

"Madame Robear."

"I guessed as much. But being voluptuous is no crime, Mad."

It is to those of us with average boobage. "Your peeps need to get a better timeline. Finding Robear on a train coming this way, hours after the murder, is a little too coincidental for me."

Werner marked "Robear's timeline" in his notebook. "Who else is on your list?" he asked, not bothering to argue my point.

"The candidate's mother, Payton's grandmother. They call her Grand-mère. Gets chauffeured around town in a powder blue stretch limo. She's here in Mystic, checking on her granddaughter. She was in my shop before I went to pick up Isobel at the station. I just didn't know then that it was her."

"I find that hard to swallow," Werner said. "Who'd kill a grandchild?"

"Who'd kill their own child? But it happens every

day, right? Instead of Grand-mère, let's call her a pushy, aggressive woman determined to see her son in the White House. A woman who'd do anything for power, even assuming her intentions were pure and she had her family's or her country's best interests at heart."

"Kill a grandkid, save a country?"

"Well, when you put it that way. Actually, I was thinking of sacrifices for the greater good, but in this context, it sounds trite and skewed, even to me."

"For argument's sake, what's Grand-mère's motive?"

I tapped my chin. "Isobel said she'd do anything to get her son elected. So, power, greed, personal aggrandizement—his station would raise hers. Check into *her* financials, why don't you?"

"Will do."

"Now," I said, sitting forward, "suppose the grand-daughter of a woman like that did something morally reprehensible, which could destroy her son's chances at getting elected—as in lousy father, lousy . . . name the office. Would that be motive enough?"

Like maybe Payton had been standing on that boat. Should politicians have call girls in the family? Should they have carhop-working girls for mothers?

Werner sharpened his pencil with an electric sharp-ener and blew on the tip as if he'd fired it like a gun. "Wouldn't Grand-mère's embezzling son have ruined his brother's chances of being elected, anyway?" Werner suggested. "I mean, no matter what the grandchildren did?"

"Not if the honest, upright candidate was the one who turned in the embezzler."

Werner placed the flat of his hands on his desk and leaned toward me. "Your mind's too busy. What are you not telling me?"

"Is this Nick's embezzlement case? Is Patrick York not the embezzler? Does it go higher up than that?"

Werner sort of growled low in his throat.

"Nuff said. But I'm working on instinct, here." And my secret psychic ability. "You'd understand if you heard Isobel talking about Grand-mère. She's powerful, she's rich, judging by her discarded Dior mink, plus she owns an island, Kingston's Vineyard, with which she plans to outshine Martha's Vineyard. Oh, and she thinks her son, Isobel's father, is the second coming of JFK."

"Sounds like she's a few vines *short* a vineyard."

"Judging by what Isobel didn't say, I think Grand-mère can be scary. How about Isobel's uncle?" I asked. "*Is* he still in prison?"

"He is," Werner said. "He needed to be told about his daughter, so I did some investigating before I made the call. The money he embezzled was never found. Maybe Payton knew where it was, and her killer was after her for it?"

"In which case, she might have needed to hide behind her cousin Isobel's identity," I suggested.

"Actually," he said, "that's a better reason for the killer to plant Isobel's ID on Payton than to make Payton a target. I mean, who asks for your ID before they kill you?"

Twenty-three

Fashion is an art. You express who you are through what you're wearing.
                                            —DANIELE DONATO

"Right," I said. "They kill you first and ask for your ID later. Give that man a cigar."

Werner rubbed his earlobe, looking pleased with himself. "Don't mind if I do." He grabbed a cigar from his desk drawer.

"Give me that." I plucked it from between his lips and snapped it in half. "Smoking kills."

He looked like a pup that lost his meaty bone. Ah, shouldn't put Werner and meaty bone in the same thought.

"Do you know how much that Cuban cost?"

"Word for word, the perfect epitaph for your headstone. 'Do you know how much that Cuban cost? My life.'" I leaned slowly over his desk, so he'd focus on my cleavage, and while his gaze was otherwise occupied, I raided his cigar drawer, breaking all three Cubans into pieces too small to smoke.

His jaw dropped.

I raised it with a finger. "I wouldn't have done it if I didn't care. Now, where were we?" I dropped the pieces into his wastebasket, dusted my hands together, and sat down. "Power and money *are* good motives, and they often go hand in hand. What happened to the money Patrick York stole?"

"Right. Marry the two motives," he said, "and you have almost everything anybody could want."

"Well, they could want revenge." I took a long sip of beer. "Suppose Payton was killed to get back at her father for the money he stole? Who did he steal it from?"

"His brother, the politician."

"Isobel's father? Didn't see that on the Net while paying for the beer."

"The very man. As for the details, we've petitioned the Feds for access to the case files." Werner tapped his mouth with a finger for a thoughtful second. "Since those voice-modulated phone calls started before Payton or Isobel arrived, it may also be a matter of mistaken identity, as in, Payton might have been the wrong target carrying the right train ticket. Where does your sister Brandy come into it? Which York girl is she friends with?"

"It's a friend of a friend thing, but Isobel, my intern. Brandy begged me to take her on. You know, if it is a case of mistaken identity, Isobel needs a bodyguard. How about Nick?" I suggested. "His ego could use a boost. He can't talk, but he can still shoot and beat the crap out of anybody."

"Except you." Werner grinned. "*You* beat the crap out of him."

"You know how that feels," I said to take the grinning starch out of him. I'd beat Werner up a time or three.

He raised both hands. "Ya got me."

"I am not proud of myself. I am really, *really* sorry I hurt Nick."

Werner rubbed the bump on his head. "I know, like you're frequently sorry you hurt me."

"For Nick to be Isobel's bodyguard," I said, "I guess he would have to live at my house."

"Damn," Werner said. "Tell you what, Isobel can move in with me."

I stood, jarred by my own reaction. "Gotta hit the ladies'. Don't need any help this time, thanks."

I shut his office door behind me, while something that smacked of jealousy followed me down the hall. I mean, so what if Isobel lived with him; I wouldn't let her, but not because of that.

From the high, transom-style open window in the ladies' room, on the E-shaped center hall of the municipal building, I saw Werner across the parking lot in his office, tipping back a bottle that might be a cola for all anybody knew.

He was also being watched by the two people standing beneath a tree outside the ladies' room: Nick and Isobel. Odd, seeing them as a pair.

I realized that I didn't like it any more than pairing Isobel and Werner in my mind. Hmm. Two men vied for my attention, and I liked it. What did that make me? The only word that came to mind was "normal."

"Wasn't my boss supposed to bring you some hot broth?" Isobel asked, as if she thought I didn't and pointed out my lack. Nah. I was imagining things.

Nick put a finger over his lips to shush her but rubbed his tummy, as if he was full. What a guy, standing up for me. Which meant he must have caught her tone as well.

She offered him a juice box from her pocket, straw included. Well, that was nice. But it meant that she was prepared to spend time with him. Adults only carried juice boxes when someone else needed them.

He took it with a surprised nod . . . which meant that he didn't expect to spend time with her. He couldn't figure it out, so she had to open it for him. Big smart FBI agent. My niece Kelsey opens those boxes and slips in the straw all the time.

"I'm following her because I'm worried about my boss," Isobel said. "She and the detective make a handsome pair, don't they?" Isobel slipped her arm through Nick's.

He looked down at their entwined arms but didn't push her away.

Was I wrong, or was she making a play for my . . . ex?

"What about you? Are you worried about her?" she asked.

A strong nod. Hard to see him in pain, knowing it to be my fault, and unable to move the facial muscles that would give away his thoughts.

"You love her, don't you?" Isobel asked.

Another affirmative nod, maybe more affirmative than the last, and it gave me a heart flutter, something to think about. Was his love for me a love forever after or the love of a BFF?

And would I want Werner to nod as affirmatively to the same question? I wasn't sure. I mean, eventually I had to choose between them, because if I didn't, what did that make me?

Besides lucky?

I supposed I'd better take stock and decide what I wanted in my . . . go-to guy? Boy toy? Life?

I couldn't really be thinking of replacing Nick. Could I?

Fact was, I couldn't think in terms of forever. Not yet. I wasn't ready. Probably came from mothering my siblings since age ten.

But I supposed I wasn't being fair to Nick or Werner. So I'd stop taking them both for granted.

Scrap silk and little bone buttons, I was guilty of doing what I accused Nick of, taking me for granted. Maybe during my years in New York, that had been mutual.

"You'd better stake your claim, then," Isobel said. "Detective Werner is, I believe, falling in love with her, too."

Nick gave her a slow, sad, affirmative nod.

Isobel leaned closer to Nick, and frankly she was ticking me off. "But you're not angry with either of them?"

First Nick nodded yes, then no. I guess that would mean he'd like to be angry, but he didn't have the right. Fact is, he hadn't staked his claim on me, either. And neither did I have a right to be upset because somebody else found him attractive, though she used me a bit like a step stool to reach him.

"So you're following her not because you're jealous but because you're trying to protect her from the guy who's after me?"

Nick nodded and moved to cross his lips with a finger, again, disengaging himself from her hold.

"I won't tell her," Isobel said.

Nick gave another half nod then repeated the sign for shh.

Nick looked sad but not jealous, probably because jealousy broke us up in the first place. Yet, after all that and a wired jaw, too, there he stood in the shadows, on my tail, just to keep an eye on me. I sighed. My hero.

My cell phone rang. The two beneath the tree turned toward the window, and I ducked and turned it off, mid-ring, wondering if Nick recognized the sound. How many people in Mystic chose the music the world most associated with the cancan as a ringtone?

On my way back through the squad room, I got a text from Brandy. Four letters: "Help."

"Billings," I said as I passed his desk. "Tell the detective I had to run. Emergency at home."

In the parking lot I whistled. "Yo, behind the tree, Isobel, let's go."

She ran over looking sheepish, brows furrowed.

"Night, Nick," I called. "Thanks for having my back."

I knew his response by heart: "I'd rather have your front."

Twenty-four

Fashions are born and they die too quickly for anyone to
learn to love them.   —BETTINA BALLARD

I drove in silence for a bit, but I couldn't help asking,
"How did you get from Mystick Falls to the police
station?"

Isobel braced herself. "Aren't you driving a little
fast?"

"It's an emergency. I got an SOS from Brandy, and
I'm trying not to imagine the worst." My father gasping
for his last breath.

"What would be the worst?" Isobel asked.

"My father or Aunt Fee being sick or hurt, anybody I
loved." Drive safely, I told myself, backing off on the
gas pedal. "Humor me to keep me sane. How did you get
to the police station?"

"I run five to ten miles a day. Didn't Brandy tell you?

I missed my run yesterday and needed to run off brownies and a Caramel Macchiato today."

I took in her Nike shorts and tank top, wondering if Nick had admired the way the athletic gear showcased her toned arms and legs. "You shouldn't have been out on the streets alone after dark, especially after that caller threatened your life. What do you say to Nick as your bodyguard?"

"I don't need—Nick? Really?"

I knew that would grab her attention. "The detective and I think you need someone to stick with you, in case the stalker-caller shows up. If you want to stay here, you'll have a bodyguard, or I'm sending you back to D.C. where you'll be safe."

"I live in New York. I happened to be visiting my grandmother in D.C. I have a place there."

You hate your grandmother, or she hates you. It's Giselle she loves. I wished I wasn't so suspicious. I really liked this girl. "I lived in New York for seven years," I said.

"I know, and you excelled in your field. That's why I wanted to learn at your creative right hand."

"I thought you didn't like your grandmother." The words slipped right out, no filter. Scrap.

Isobel bit her lip, then she gave me a sheepish grin. "Doesn't mean I care to be cut from the will."

"I think you'd be safer with Nick as your bodyguard. I'll ask him if he can do it. It'll make him feel useful while he's healing. Having your attention and protecting you will also make him feel more like the hunky FBI agent he is."

"FBI? I mean, he's so cute. Who'd guess? Are you sure you want us spending time together?"

"Nick and I have been on again, off again since junior high," I said. "We're off right now."

"You make it sound temporary."

"Maybe I think it is," I said, considering. "As a couple, we're unsettled, to say the least."

"So you have one of those bungee-type relationships?"

"Yes, and the bungee cord is usually on fire, me breathing smoke and getting whiplash. Take him off my hands. Please."

"Permanently?"

That sent a knife point to my chest. "I'm not asking you to marry him; just let him keep you safe while you're here." I parked on a dime and ran into the house.

"Brandy, is Dad okay?"

"I'm fine," my father said, "if overrun with women, again, like the good old days."

I put my fists on my hips. "Brandy, why did you call for help? You scared ten years off my life."

"Panic," Brandy said. "Cort wants me to move in early tomorrow, and he's having a few potential donors in for a dinner party tomorrow night so they can meet me."

"But that's good, right?"

"That's bad. I don't want Cort to see me like this. I

don't have any daytime clothes, never mind dinner party clothes."

"I had to fight with you to get new clothes and now you're—"

"Begging?" Brandy asked on a chuckle. "I was working you, Sis. I knew you'd outfit me. I didn't miss the fact that I met Cort wearing something of Mom's that *you* picked out. Can you go back to the shop tonight and find a few quick pieces for me so I can start being a proper development director tomorrow and attend a dinner party in my honor at Vancortland House tomorrow night?"

Can *you* go back to the shop tonight? she'd asked. Not can *we*?

"This reminds me of a quote." My father chuckled. "'Women thrive on novelty and are easy meat for the commerce of fashion. Men prefer old pipes and torn jackets.'"

"Well, *you* certainly prefer them, Dad," I said. "I think your smoking jacket is old enough to vote."

"Anthony Burgess spoke those words, and I'm telling you, he was right!"

"Sure he was. Isobel, you want to come to the shop with me and Brandy?"

"I'd like to crash," she said, "if that's okay with everyone?"

Werner knocked and walked in, Nick behind him.

"What brought you two here? Together?"

"Your quick escape," Werner said. "Billings said you beat a quick path out of the police station due to a family emergency. Nick saw you running across the parking lot, calling for Isobel, and once we compared notes, we decided to follow you here."

"Well, good," I said. "Nick, I want to hire you to be Isobel's bodyguard until we find the voice-modulated caller who said she should be dead."

Nick scribbled on the notebook he kept in his jeans pocket. "Yes, but you have to keep me in the loop."

"I won't interfere with your FBI work?" Isobel asked.

"On leave," Nick wrote.

"Perfect," I said. "You'll have to move in here, though. Is that a problem?"

Nick winked and grinned at me.

Werner elbowed him.

"Nick, you can have Alex's room, across from Sherry's," I said, "which is where Isobel is staying. You'll be in the room next door to my father's, as you might remember."

My father chuckled. "Don't threaten him with my presence. Alex, Tricia, and the baby are on their way— they'll take my room—and I'm moving to Fiona's. I'll come back every day, but I'm out of here late evenings and nights, so I can get the kind of peace a man of my years needs."

Fiona's eyes twinkled. "A man of your years."

Such a loaded statement.

"I didn't think Alex and Tricia were coming until the weekend," I said.

"Alex now has to go to Washington, D.C., to teach Nick's classes at an FBI conference this week, and he wants Tricia and the baby to be in good hands. That way, he can just meet them back here for the fund-raiser."

I hung my head. "Sheesh, you break one jaw and throw your entire family into a tizzy."

"You're not kidding, Sis," Alex said, pushing open the door with his backside, juggling luggage and dragging baby furniture behind him.

Alex's wife, Tricia, came in and handed Kelsey to me. "That's what you get," she said, "for beating up your boyfriend. Aunt duty."

"No," Werner said. "Mad and Nick broke up."

Everyone eyed him.

He lost his delight in the news and backed up a step. "Just the facts, ma'am."

Kelsey opened her arms to Nick, who took her but tried to keep his jaw a safe distance from her probing fingers, though he needn't have bothered. Kelsey recognized a boo-boo when she saw one. She pointed toward his purpling jaw with a small finger. "I kiss it better?" she asked.

Nick nodded.

Kelsey planted her baby lips gently on his jaw. "All better," the little one said, patting Nick's shoulder as if she were taking care of him.

Nick cupped my baby niece's head and touched his lips to her brow.

And I felt an arrow shoot straight to my heart. Had I lost the possibility of having this wonderful man in my life? Had I lost the opportunity of a lifetime?

Twenty-five

Artistic creativity is a whirlpool of imagination that swirls in the depths of the mind.
                                        —ROBERT TOTH

"We'd best go get Brandy's new clothes," Werner said. "Nick, this'll give you a chance to hang out with Alex and his wife for the evening while Isobel rests. I'll escort Mad to the shop and act as *her* bodyguard."

Brandy smiled, a rare sight. "And I'll stay here and play Auntie so Tricia can rest."

I couldn't believe her. "You really don't care what I dress you in, do you, Bran?"

"Nope. I trust you."

"Okay, then." I waved at Nick, and he gave me a wink that I could practically read, a reminder that he's my go-to guy.

Werner raised a saluting hand. "See you all tomorrow. Night, Mr. Cutler, Ms. Sullivan. You probably won't be up when we get back."

"Or here," my father said beneath his breath, and I chuckled.

Nick handed me a note. "Go through OLD clothes when Eve or I can help."

"Nonsense," Werner said, reading it over my shoulder and thinking nothing of the capital OLD. "I can help her."

"Good night, Detective," my father said, his eyes narrow, his expression rather sternly protective and fatherly as he watched Werner's hand at my back.

While we headed toward the car, Eve called my cell phone, looking for details about Nick's jaw. "You heard," I said. "I want to hear about your weekend, too, but not now. I need to go get some outfits for Brandy the development director and Brandy the sophisticate."

I frowned and looked at my phone before I brought it back up to my ear. "Will you stop laughing? I'm serious. Sure you can, but Werner's with me. Nah, he wouldn't mind if you came along in your pj's. Would Kyle?"

"Yes, I would," Werner said. "Tell her to stay with Kyle. I'm all the help you'll need."

"Kyle agrees with you," I said as I put my phone away. "Are you taking your own car, or are you coming with me in mine?"

"Give me your keys. I've never driven an Element."

I tossed my keys his way.

He opened the passenger door for me and gave me a hand up. "Such a gentleman."

"Please, don't spoil the moment with snark."

I said nothing more until he settled himself in the driver's side.

He turned the key in the ignition, and my car got smaller inside, intimate, with Werner in the driver's seat, like this was a date or something. "You misunderstood," I said. "I *like* being treated like a lady."

"Glad to hear it. I like not getting beat up."

He grabbed my hand across the space between the seats and squeezed.

We'd shared a thermonuclear kiss, and I was having heart palpitations because he held my hand on purpose.

Unaware of my heightened senses, he pulled into the Vintage Magic parking lot.

My motion detector lights went on along the front and right side of my building, which made Dante step into an upstairs window. Without windows downstairs— because this was an old carriage house, and I didn't want sunshine fading my vintage treasures, anyway—my friendly ghost wasn't likely to spook me with a face-to-face. No, the only windows on the lower level were small squares, high behind the horse stalls, aka dressing rooms, and I liked it that way.

Not that Werner could see Dante watching us.

Then again, Werner was continually surprising me.

"I want to bring Brandy a good selection," I said. "I hope we find enough for the next few days, but my right arm has been sore all day, maybe from when I blacked out this morning and you caught me up. If I point out the items I want, would you mind reaching up to take them off the racks for me? And would you carry them?"

"You scared me this morning, Mad. I didn't mean to hurt you. I apologize."

I *hated* making him feel guilty. "You know what? Bet I did it breaking Nick's jaw last night."

Werner sighed with relief. "Now that makes me feel a whole lot better."

Don't know why I didn't come up with a better whopper right away. Anyway, I lied through my teeth so I didn't have to touch the clothes, take a chance on getting a reading, zone, and flake out in front of Werner. I pretty much believed that having him see me do that more than once a day would be too much.

Inside, he stopped me from turning on anything but indirect lights and hooked his iPod to my speakers. "Memories are Made of This" flooded the shop.

He took me in his arms as purposefully as he'd taken my hand, and he waltzed me like a professional dancer around my "roller skating" area.

"Bravo, Detective," I said, breathless. "I could get used to this."

"I was hoping you could."

"Que Sera, Sera" followed. What will be and all that . . .

"You found a fifties station?"

"I have a fifties compilation."

I couldn't argue with that. When we waltzed to "The Wayward Wind," I felt wayward, and he led the way like a pro. "Is this a date?"

"No," he said. "I'd prepare better for a date. We've just gone AWOL for a bit. We'll find a wardrobe for Brandy soon enough. This is just a short trip to the fifties that we can appreciate together."

"How many fifties songs do you have in that thing?"

"Thousands," he said with a wink.

Bill Haley & His Comets' "Rock Around the Clock" turned Werner into a cool cat. I got twirled and dipped, so in sync with him, you'd have thought we practiced for hours.

"You're awesome," I said, so close to his hard bod . . . I wanted to stay and learn more.

This man is no wiener, I thought. What an injustice I'd perpetrated, giving him that name as a kid.

"In college," he said, "we had one of those jock-brilliant football coaches who thought dancing would help us move."

Werner had the physique of a football player: broad shoulders, small waist, tight tush. Handsome, with the command of a dynamic leader, all belying the graceful way he moved on the dance floor.

Nick, on the other hand, stood nearly as tall, darker haired, solid and more compact, swarthy, with aquiline features and warrior-like fighting skills, a hunka-hunka Italian stallion.

Werner caught my eye. Had I been quiet for too long? "Go, coach!" I said.

Twenty-six

The dress is a vase which the body follows. My clothes are like
modules in which bodies move.　　　　—PIERRE CARDIN

"I could dance all night," I said, stopping to catch my
breath, "but we need to grab Brandy's wardrobe before it
gets too late. I'm beat after assaulting you last night. You?"

"I'll admit it," Werner said. "I'm bruised and beat,
but, Mad, come dancing with me sometime, will you?
I've never had such a great partner. Seriously, we'll
make a night of it. No strings."

"As friends? I'd like that."

"It's Raining Men" played in my head. Sometimes I
thought that maybe I *wanted* to fall for Werner, but I
couldn't deny that Nick, my gorgeous go-to guy, since
like forever, meant the world to me.

Until I made up my mind, I was going to enjoy the
ride and consider myself one lucky girl.

Werner dipped me. Lucky, yeah. That's my story, and I'm sticking to it.

But when the music slowed, I straightened and stepped back, a little less seduced by the music, a bit more aware of crossing a line. "We have to get Brandy's clothes together."

Werner sighed and removed his hands from my person. "Your wish and all that," he said.

"Fine." I pointed to the clothes on Grand-mère's rack. "Grab that plum jacket with the shawl collar, the plum pencil skirt, and plaid box pleat skirt. She can mix and match them and fit completely in, between now and Saturday, with the fund-raiser's fifties theme. Pencil skirt for evening, plaid box pleats for day wear."

Werner grabbed when I nodded, or moved on if I shook my head. "Like I know what a pencil shawl is," he grumbled.

"You wanted to come along and help me."

"I wanted to come and dance with you."

I raised a chiding brow, and he had the sense to look sheepish.

I let him off the hook. "At home, I have a Hermès reversible scarf print jacket, and I can't believe I'm doing this, but I'll *generously* lend it to her while she's in town. I can find twenty skirts to go with that; the colors are so vibrant."

"Please," Werner begged. "Spare me the details." He set the clothes down on the counter. "Come, dance with me. I like this next one a lot."

"Running Bear" started with a Native American beat and didn't require the traditional rock and roll but a slow, close, rock and waltz.

When Werner crossed his arms above his chest, I did the same, and we circled each other, keeping to the beat.

"I love this song," I said.

"White Dove, shush!" He pulled me into his arms when the couple met in the middle of the river, as if to keep *me* from drowning, then the beat picked up, and he started to twirl me.

My front door slammed.

"Say cheese," a stranger said, snapping a picture and disappearing as fast as he appeared.

Werner let go of me to chase the photographer.

I lost my balance, reached out, grabbed a rack, and took it and Grand-mère's vintage clothes down with me.

I began to swirl away as soon as my head hit the floor. I saw Werner's concern as he came for me, then I found myself sitting on the back of a convertible like a beauty queen in a Saint Patty's Day parade. Not that anybody could see me.

Grand-mère roller-skated across a parking lot in front of a red and yellow checkered diner with blue and green neon trim. Wow, the fifties were colorful.

She carried a tray high in one hand, showing off her figure to perfection, and didn't she know it. On the tray: a frosted mug of root beer, a couple of plates with burgers and fries. She went to the turquoise T-bird, white top, one car over. "Peachy car," she said, hooking a tray to the open window. Her name tag said Betty at this diner, but it was still Grand-mère in her youth, whatever name she used.

"A nifty fifty-seven roadster, is Beulah," said Slick, his hair greased back. "Want a ride?" *Wink, wink.*

"Gotta work." She looked around, making a point of appearing disinterested.

I got a bead on her view, my own limited by my location, but I saw a couple Corvettes, a pink and black Rambler, and a woodie station wagon. I noticed they all had Rhode Island license plates and there was no mistaking the scent of the sea. Besides, a sign on the diner said Chowder and Clam Cakes, and you could only buy clam cakes in Rhode Island.

Slick in the T-bird cleared his throat.

Betty focused on her customer. "Will there be anything else?" she asked, playing coy.

"Sure," he said. "I want an answer. Nine tonight. The Palms. West side." He slipped Betty some money.

She checked her take as she rode by me: at least two one hundred dollar bills and another motel key. I wondered what she would have to do for double the loot. Or heck, maybe the guy at the last place gave her a down payment. What did I know? The names of the motels that went with the keys had fired my imagination.

Scrap. Had Grand-mère truly been a hooker in her day? One with a heart of gold, maybe, but she must have loved the thrill of it, because she whooped.

So the old lady and one of her granddaughters were both hookers. What did that have to do with Payton's death? I'd like to know.

I heard rather than saw the T-bird peel out of the lot. A second screech, close on the rubber Slick laid, made me wonder who'd followed him.

A new nickel had gone into the jukebox, because the loudspeakers blared, ". . . all I have to do is dream."

And dream I did.

Twenty-seven

It's not what you wear—it's how you take it off.
—AUTHOR UNKNOWN

The music stopped. Time did not.

I entered this vision *inside* Betty's skin, nervous as a frog in a frying pan, wearing the banded yellow sleeveless boatneck swing dress with red flower-topped, opentoed shoes I wished I'd found in the trunk.

I slipped the key in the lock. Room 203. The Palms. West side.

But when the force of turning it pushed the door open, I stilled, my heart beating double time, until I reached inside and flipped on the light, and my heart beat faster.

Two men occupied the room.

Slick, the rich *chosen* father of my unborn child, my ticket out of hell, damn it, lay unconscious on the floor.

The man sprawled on the bed, dirty cowboy boots defiling a white bedspread, swore a familiar blue streak and swigged cheap whiskey. "Thought you could get away with it, didn't you, Liz?"

I, as Elizabeth Kingston York, raised my chin. "Our boys have to eat, and I don't see you bringing home any bacon."

He threw the empty bottle at the wall where it shattered, making me jump, getting my attention the way he liked it, with me cowering.

This time, I wouldn't give him the satisfaction. I raised my chin, hoping he read my defiance. "What a husband," I said. "Drunk as usual."

"With a hooker for a wife, do you blame me?"

"You've been drunk for ten years. I've been hooking for five."

"What do they pay you?" he asked. "Because you're not bringing home the bacon, either, not to me."

I ignored that. "Fifty to be here, and another fifty . . . after." Grand-mère's satisfaction was a little too satisfying for Madeira Cutler's comfort.

Her husband shot off the bed. "You lying bitch! That guy said he gave you two C notes, up front."

Grand-mère took a small step back, then another. "So why'd you ask?"

When her husband produced a flask from his jean jacket and took a swig, she pulled a revolver from her purse.

She hit the light switch, a breeze swung the door shut, and my vision turned to night blindness.

After a sensation of floating out of my body—mine, Madeira Cutler's—the sound of sirens in the distance became the wind whistling through trees, and leaves swirling around headstones, the last leaves of the season, crisp and disintegrating beneath my hands.

I knelt at the edge of a shallow grave, at the far edge of a cemetery, watching a woman put all her muscle into wielding a shovel, the veil from her black straw hat pulled down to hide as much of her face as possible.

Her feet were bare, her red toenails scuffed and filthy, her black swing skirt dress, with high neck and long sleeves, as much a disguise, at this hour, as her hat.

Something covered my mouth and nose, and I struggled to breathe, but I breathed better with it on.

The gravedigger looked around, firmed her lips, and kept digging. Whose grave? I wondered. Not mine?

My scream evolved as did I.

I sat enveloped in the Dior mink coat on a Ferris wheel beside Monsieur Debonair, tall, dark, and handsome, a French accent in his speaking voice and kissing skill.

I didn't know him, but I knew the people walking through the amusement park below us wore new millennium–style clothes.

Time had fast-forwarded. Not one of Grand-mère's dates or nightmares, then.

It didn't matter. I was no voyeur in this vision but the call girl herself, whichever York cousin I might be.

I looked around to get my bearings and saw a replica of the Eiffel Tower, realized as we stepped from the Ferris wheel that the people around us spoke French.

This must be one of boat girl's "calls." She'd go anywhere in the world, evidently, and she treated her clients with compliant familiarity, given Monsieur's practiced hands, everywhere. "Now to my château," he said.

Oy!

We drove through what appeared to be the French countryside and passed a sign for Provence. OMG, if only I could enjoy this, instead of hoping it would end before we consummated our contract.

"So you know my boss," I said by way of leading conversation.

"She is a gem."

A she—I hadn't expected that. But, sure, it made sense, a high-class madam. "I enjoyed the first-class flight out here. She said you were generous."

"We shall both reap your journey's rewards," he said. *"Seulement toi et moi."*

Yeah right. *Moi* would rather stay out of it, *s'il vous* please.

"There she is, my home," said my client. "Château Sevigny. Tomorrow, a tour of my vineyard. The weekend, she will sing. You are, how you say, a masterpiece well worth your price. *Très jolie."*

Ducky for me.

"What shall I call you?" I asked.

"You may call me Anatole, or *mon amour*. And I will call you *ma belle*, *oui*?"

Non! "*Oui, Anatole.*"

There she went acting submissive again, not at all like Isobel, though I supposed acting was the operative word.

Anatole Sevigny—since I assumed his château carried the family name—parked his Daimler in a cluster of trees and slid toward me, his hands getting friendlier beneath the mink, his mouth coming for mine, a hungry, I-can't-wait gleam in his expression.

I struggled to shed the mink, praying that *toujours l'amour* hunk-du-jour would disappear with it.

Twenty-eight

Sometimes there are two very opposite directions, and we go
with the stronger one at the end. It's an impulse thing, like,
"Oh, I love both so much, but it's got to be one or the other
because the two don't work together." —MARC JACOBS

I touched my head, heard a softer "All I Have to Do Is
Dream," and opened my eyes to find Werner stroking the
hair from my brow with a gentle hand.

We weren't alone. Paramedics surrounded me. Taking my pulse, monitoring a drip solution.

I took off my oxygen mask and my elbow slid across
something silky.

A painful tilt of my head revealed the source. I tossed
the damned mink away from me. No wonder I'd seen
that vision.

"Mad," Werner said. "Your teeth were chattering. We
couldn't warm you up. I'd turned up the heat, but only
the mink worked."

"That's what you think." I tried to sit up.

Werner pushed me down, his hands on my shoulders.

"We're going to take you to the hospital, Mad," said Johnny Shields, school chum, paramedic, and volunteer firefighter. "For observation."

"No hospital," I said so emphatically, my head hurt with both words. I touched where it hurt and turned to Werner. "My prune matches yours."

"I'm really, really sorry," he said.

"You didn't know I'd go twirling into outer space, now did you?"

"You need to come to the hospital, Mad," Johnny said, Tunney watching me with concern over Johnny's shoulder.

Tunney Lague, local meat cutter, ace purveyor of gossip, great cook, good friend, giver of fun pony rides, albeit years ago, a fixture around Mystic.

"Tunney, not one word about this to my dad," I said. "Not to anyone, not even your cousins in Canada. This is a medical issue. You show up, you take on patient-doctor confidentiality. Right, Johnny?"

Johnny shrugged, trying to hide his smile. "I'd listen to her, Tunney."

"I'd rather know she's okay," Tunney said. "You sure you won't go, Mad? C'mon, to make this old warhorse happy?"

I folded my arms. "I know my rights. You can't make me go if I don't want to. Werner called you without my permission."

"You were out cold," Johnny said.

"Do I have a concussion?" I asked.

Johnny shook his head. "No, but you're making it a case of good news, bad news. You always were a stubborn one."

"I've got enough people to watch me not sleep tonight. If my eyes dilate under a flashlight, I'll let them take me in."

A paramedic I didn't know gave me something to sign.

Werner looked worried, guilty, and half-annoyed as he saw our neighbors out, professionals and gossips alike.

"Lock the door," I called and had to hold my head so it wouldn't spin into space again, this time without me.

No wonder I'd had a string of visions, I thought, looking at Grand-mère's clothes scattered around me.

Good thing I hadn't hung the roller skates by their laces. I would have needed stitches.

Werner returned looking like he might want to spank me or worse.

I raised a hand. "When you yell, don't forget I've been injured and that my head hurts."

He got me up and to the fainting couch, then he sat behind me, his feet on the floor, his arms coming hard around me.

I laid the non-bruised side of my head against his chest. "I'd look up at you if I could stand the pain."

"I'm so very sorry."

"I know. Lytton, you don't look very comfortable like that. No need to be a martyr."

"I'm exactly where I want to be. You took twenty years off my life, and it's my fault."

I closed my eyes at the earnest statement. I rather liked feeling treasured and not being taken for granted. Werner did care for me, and, yes, I could say that I cared for him, in my own way. But I also sincerely cared for Nick.

"Two Guys on a String." Wasn't *that* a fifties song?

Maybe I shouldn't rule out a concussion; my discussion with myself was getting weird.

Soft spinning slubs, I was a regular Eve Meyers, with hot guys coming out the dye vat. Surely, I could inspire a new song: "Mirth Angel" or "Jailhouse Crock."

Twenty-nine

Design is the search for a magical balance between business and art; art and craft; intuition and reason; concept and detail; playfulness and formality; client and designer.

—VALERIE PETTIS

"Did you ever catch the guy who took our picture?" I asked Werner.

"No, he had a car waiting for him across the street in the bookstore parking lot."

"Even with *my* track record, a guy running in to take my picture is weird."

"Our picture." Werner spoke with an unmistakable, deep-down satisfaction.

I touched his face and startled him.

"Mad, you're like ice," he said, chafing my hands.

"Nice." I shivered, though I wasn't sure why, and Werner moved to warm me with his arms along mine; then he stretched out and occupied almost the same space on the couch, his hand warming me everywhere, making me toasty deep down, inside and out.

"Are you sure you wouldn't like the mink over you?" he asked.

"Hermès, no!" My teeth began to chatter. Vision overload, I thought. A lot like short-circuiting in cold storage.

I felt breathless like in the car when he took my hand. Strangely intimate. A little scared. Shivery with . . . guilt?

Then he leaned in and kissed me. His lips held the kind of warmth I sought, so I made sure to keep them where they were, against mine. A chaste kiss, by new millennium standards, though it lasted, causing an inner warmth I craved. In the back of my mind, I knew this was less about romance and more about me being a heat-seeking missile right now. I'd have to remember to tell Werner.

One of us groaned. Maybe both of us. We came up for air at the same time, stared with shock into each other's eyes, and he swooped in for more.

I squeaked like we'd been caught when his cell phone rang.

He swore but answered, straightened, sat up, and listened as if to catch every word. Then he hung up.

"We got a faxed copy of the paperwork on the York embezzlement case," he said leaning back against the fainting couch and pulling me against him.

"And?" I asked, eager to hear.

"It seems Quincy York blew the whistle on his brother, then he made a public and televised plea for leniency at Patrick's circus of a trial."

"Hmm," I said. "Not that I'm like my father, but . . . that reminds me of an old saying: 'When a tree falls in the woods and nobody hears, does it make a sound?'"

Werner frowned. "Say what?"

"I mean, the first selectman candidate of Kingston's Vineyard made sure the world heard a tree fall, one way or another. He showed off both the extent of his assets and his kindness."

I tried to phrase it better. "Quincy York revealed himself as rich, law-abiding, and vulnerable to being taken advantage of by his family. And he ended up looking generous, righteous, and understanding."

Werner nodded slowly. "So you think it was about what the world saw, not what really happened?"

I shrugged. "It's just a theory."

"A logical one," Werner said. "When the candidate turned in his brother, the world saw a man 'doing the right thing' with deep regret. They might have seen him as a man they'd want to vote for."

"I think the entire York family should go on our suspect list."

"Even your Isobel?" he asked.

"To be fair, yes. And Giselle, too."

"Isobel's twin is an official missing person. Nobody's seen her for months."

Except maybe the clients who hire her. "I hate that she's missing. One twin would inherit more without the other."

"Face it, Mad, they both have motive, if Giselle's still alive."

"Or dead. Also, the twins stand to inherit more from Grand-mère, with their first cousin out of the picture."

"Motive for Payton's murder is starting to crop up everywhere," he said.

"Lytton, would you let me examine the clothes she was wearing when she died?"

"Why?"

"I *know* clothes. I studied them, fabrics and construction, thread types, workmanship; they all say a lot about the wearer. I can practically read clothes. I might see something a forensics scientist would miss."

"Fine, but you'll have to come to the station around nine in the morning, before the forensic lab's ten o'clock pickup."

"I'll be there."

A member of the Mystick Falls police force walked in.

"Stevens?" Werner said, getting off the fainting couch, taking off his suit jacket and setting it over my shoulders. "What are *you* doing here?"

"I picked the short straw, sir."

"What?"

"I lost the bet, so I'm here to tell you—That is, we

thought you needed to know, Sarge, that the deceased's uncle, Candidate York, commandeered the Pearl Seahorse for his on-site campaign headquarters."

"The people of Mystic aren't even his voters," Werner said.

I tugged on the leg of Werner's slacks. "Bigger picture, remember? Governor's mansion. White House."

"For the love of—I suppose he'll be easier to investigate close by," Werner conceded, giving away his agitation by jiggling the keys in his pocket.

"His campaign manager will be closer, too," I added.

Stevens rolled his hat in his hand. "After you left, sir, we had to send an officer down to direct traffic, sir, while York and his entourage moved in. He bought out the hotel. The owners had to find their guests other accommodations."

Stevens took a step back when Werner cleared his throat. "I have to say it again, or go and grab somebody by the throat: They're just making our jobs easier."

"I don't know, sir, they've already held a press conference."

"Please tell me it was to tell the world they were here."

Stevens shook his head and backed up another step. "No, sir. Basically, they said Quincy York's niece had been murdered, and York is here to oversee the Mystick Falls Police investigation."

"Oversee?" Werner snapped. "And he used the word 'murdered'?"

"York really meant 'profit from,'" I said. "You know, snatch the sympathy votes while the snatching's good?"

"A servant of the people just told a murderer, or three, that the police are on their tail! Is York an idiot or what?"

Werner charged over to Stevens, and the poor officer jumped and about scuttled out of range while looking to me for help.

"Now, Lytton," I said.

Werner wagged a finger at his beleaguered officer. "If I hear as much as a snicker about me and Miss Cutler at the station, Stevens, or outside the station, you have parking meter duty every winter until you retire."

"Yes, sir. Never saw a thing, sir."

"Thank you, Stevens," I said, getting up to stand beside Werner while Stevens went out and got into his squad car. Then I closed the shop door and leaned against it, putting myself between the mad detective and his short-straw minion.

"You can't hold Stevens responsible if you hear anything about us. Tunney saw how worried you were. A liaison between us is already on the fast track to gossip central."

Werner groaned, but "The Purple People Eater" started to play, fitting, after this wild wack-a-doo day, and the music made him smile.

During "Catch a Falling Star," he lowered his mouth to mine, and for the first time, I raised my arms to slide them around his neck and hold on. As an experiment.

Necking. That's what we were doing. Good old-fashioned necking, until "The Great Pretender" came on and I stepped from his arms.

I turned off the iPod and homed in on Grand-mère's trunk. Why had she packed up those clothes in particular? Why bury a decade, so to speak?

And what, pray tell, happened to Grand-père?

Thirty

On the subject of dress, almost no one, for one or another reason, feels truly indifferent: if their own clothes do not concern them, somebody else's do. —ELIZABETH BOWEN

I came down my father's stairs the next morning to a houseful of family and friends at the breakfast table.

"I just set Brandy up with a new wardrobe," I said, "and she looks splendid in almost everything I brought from the shop. Very few discards."

"Not counting the pieces you lent her from your own collection," Isobel said. "You're a good sister."

"She is," Sherry said as I kissed her cheek.

"No, don't get up." I squeezed her shoulders. "You've got too much to carry, there. You're *sure* it's not twins?"

Sherry chuckled as she gave Alex's little Kelsey another piece of toast.

"Brandy looks like a successful businesswoman," I

added, "and she's got a few outfits that make her look like one hell of a development director."

Nick slapped a folded newspaper into my hand, no mornin' nod or eye twinkle.

Stumped, I opened the paper and gasped. The headline: "Detective Chooses Two-Step Over Investigation," topped a big-ascot picture of the two of us dancing.

The news story went on to elaborate the ways in which Detective Sergeant Lytton Werner was too busy with the owner of the local secondhand shop—I gasped in indignation—to do anything about finding the killer of Candidate Quincy York's dearest niece, Payton.

"His *only* niece," I said. "So, the photographer came from campaign headquarters. Here's an unpaid political ad, if ever I saw one."

I caught Nick watching me. *That's* why he gave me the cold shoulder, and why he let Isobel fawn over him at breakfast. Payback, which I deserved. And I wouldn't insult him by trying to explain the fifties music thing.

Funny how Isobel's father, the candidate, didn't seem worried about his twins' welfare, in light of his niece's death. Didn't care that he hadn't seen Giselle in months or that Payton died disguised as Isobel, which might mean that Isobel was being hunted by a killer. If he cared at all for them, he would have used his money to send people looking for Giselle to make sure she was okay, and he would have hired a bodyguard for Isobel. And he wouldn't have made a three-ring circus of the investigation, putting them both in more danger in the event the murder was a case of mistaken identity.

"Isobel, has your father called you since he moved to town?"

She looked up. "He moved to town?"

"Yes, campaign staff and all, but you're safer in Nick's care living here. Don't let him talk you into moving to the Pearl Seahorse."

"Don't worry." She mocked the suggestion with a snarky chuckle. "He won't try."

Before I could comment, Brandy came down the keeping-room stairs and gathered a small admiration society doling out comments and compliments. She held herself as if she felt like a new woman, a woman in charge, because she looked like one.

A minute later, Cort, Sherry's father-in-law and Brandy's host for the week, kissed Brandy's brow in greeting. He gave the same attention to Sherry, about to bear his second grandchild—he had sole custody of his first, little Vanessa, whose father died serving in Iraq. His fiancée, Amber—Vanessa's mother and Cort's daughter—was doing an extended stint in a psychiatric facility.

Cort grabbed Brandy's bags.

As for her, she looked like a new woman.

I never thought I'd see the day Brandy could befriend a millionaire non-philanthropist, unless she knew something about Cort I didn't.

Before she preceded him out the door, she came to give me a thank-you hug. She'd never held so tight. As for me, thinking of Isobel and her distant family, neither had I held so tight or appreciated Brandy so much.

"Good luck, sweetie. Call me if you need me," I said. "Fund-raiser's right on schedule, though. Everybody's picking up their fifties formals for the big evening event. Some chose fifties day wear for the afternoon garden party/car show."

"You, too," Brandy said. "Good luck sleuthing." She eyed the newspaper, dancing picture side up. "Good luck all around."

Several of us watched Brandy and Cort drive away, though we weren't the entire family, since Tricia was sleeping in, and my dad had yet to return from Fiona's.

"I'm off to the morgue," I said. "If anyone cares. Werner's going to let me look at the clothes Payton was wearing."

Isobel sat straighter. "That's smart. Nobody knows clothes better than you do."

Had I told her that Payton died wearing rags?

"Detective Werner told me Payton's outfit seemed odd," Isobel said, furrowing her brow. "Or my dad told me, or Ruben did."

Ambiguity was so not welcome at this point in the investigation.

Werner seemed to be waiting for me as he paced his office.

He whistled when he saw me.

Besides Isobel, he was the first to appreciate my sixties Geoffrey Beene mint green linen slit-neck swing dress, paired with bow-topped natural python platform pumps.

"You look like a meadow in a bottle," he said. "A real tonic."

"Bet you say that to all the glamazons."

He winced, because those had been fighting words in third grade. His words.

"That's a compliment these days," I assured him. "Don't worry, no more name-calling. What's got you so happy?"

"You can tell, hey? With Nick's FBI connections, he tracked down the money Patrick York embezzled."

"The fortune that went missing a few years ago? That's big. So that *was* Nick's case with its tentacles around the throat of our case? I guessed correctly."

"Yep. After tracing a series of York holding and dummy companies incorporated under fake names, nonexistent subsidiaries, and subdivisions, Nick and I sort of found it at the same time in Ruben Rickard's own convoluted financials."

"I knew Rickard was too cocky. When did you and Nick do all this?"

"Almost all night last night. Why?"

"Just wondering. So how does it help solve Payton's death?"

"Oddly enough, Payton's name was on one of Rickard's fake companies."

"So you think they were embezzling partners and they let her father go to prison for their crime?"

"That might be jumping the gun, but it's a distinct possibility we'd need to prove."

"I must say that I've lost a bit of sympathy for her, but may I see her clothes, anyway?"

"The forensics lab came for her body at eight, couple hours earlier than expected, but I held the clothes back for you. I can messenger them over when you're done. No need to go to the morgue; they're in my office, but you have to wear latex gloves to touch them."

Gloves to touch thrift store throwaways? It might work for the future, to keep me from having public visions, but would it work? I mean, how would I look fitting a dress wearing latex gloves? Like a freak of nature?

On the other hand, I might *need* a reading. How do I pull that off wearing gloves?

When, as I feared, I got nothing from the clothes, I skimmed my exposed wrist above the gloves, along the peach peasant blouse. As I did, I heard "Good, the bitch'll look like crap in that," in a deep, *modulated* voice.

It all happened in a blip, and I barely blinked, though I wasn't sure when Werner got so close. I turned to him. "Somebody went Dumpster diving for these. Cheap, no personality. Definitely not something a York would wear, any York. My instinct is that she was being demeaned on purpose, maybe controlled, especially on the train, possibly with the trace drugs found in her system."

"Good hypothesis," Werner said, "because the trace drug, while it could make her easily manageable, couldn't kill her, and it would have been taken in pill form. But there's a single recent needle mark in her arm with no drug to account for it being there."

"What requires a needle to inject but leaves no trace?" I asked.

"Air," Werner said. "Insulin, because it occurs naturally in the body, though too much can kill, like certain minerals. I'm sure forensics has a long list of injectable invisible killers."

"Speaking of injections, Grand-mère's a diabetic," I said. "There were old needles in the top tray of the trunk."

"Did you touch them?"

"Of course n . . . no, actually."

"I'm gonna send somebody over to dust that trunk and everything in it for prints. Should have done it before."

"I *need* the roller skates for Saturday."

"Hold that thought. I gotta take this call." He listened and hung up. "This is odd, but a transporter from the forensics lab is here for Payton."

"I thought they came two hours ago."

"So did we all. Whoever took her body was evidently not from the lab we hired. The medical examiner said the early paperwork was in order. Two people came for her then, a male driver and his female intern."

I indicated his door. "Should we go talk to the morgue staff, see if we can get a description of the drivers?"

"We can do that if the morgue surveillance cameras don't show us anything. With cameras at different angles, we can usually get a license plate and ID the drivers."

I followed him to the morgue for a copy of the visitors' log. "I want you to know that no blame is being placed," he told his peeps, which they seemed to appreciate.

I followed a silent Werner to a room with a bank of wall monitors.

Werner introduced me to Officer Zales, at the controls, and handed him the log copy. "Right there," Werner said, pointing to the second to the last entry. "To the minute, pull up the surveillance."

"Of course, both drivers are wearing billed uniform hats, pulled down to cover their eyes, and dark glasses," I said as the video came up from different angles on six screens.

Werner jingled the change in his pocket, a sign of tension. "The driver's moving like he knows where our cameras are," Werner remarked. "He's rubbing his face, scratching his nose. Whoops, there go his keys, and he picks them up in a forward surge until he's out of camera range."

"What about the female intern?" I asked. "She's staying in the car. Is that normal?

"Never mind," I said. "She's getting out on the passenger side, coming around but moving before she rounds the vehicle to grab the door handle with her left hand, while keeping her back to us, and she stays that way while the body's slipped inside."

Werner swore. "There's a dodge. They returned to the front seat on the far side and he's getting in on her side, cap down until they pull away."

"Go back," I said. "I think I caught a glimpse of . . . there she is! She glanced in the center rearview mirror, see, then the side mirror. Red hair. Too much makeup. Back up and watch her hand to her hair. It's not a smoothing or a comb-through but a tug. She's wearing a wig."

Werner whistled. "Good call, Mad."

"Officer Zales, I don't suppose you can do a *Bones*- or *CSI*-type TV miracle and superimpose her mouth and nose from the center mirror and her right cheek and half jaw and lips from the side mirror into that full reflection of her on the windshield?"

Zales looked like I had two heads.

"Then can you mesh it somehow so we can get a light/dark facial view?"

Zales raised a brow and quirked his lips. "Since TV

equipment is probably fake, I can't quite pull that off. But since I'm a genius, give me fifteen to be brilliant."

Werner bought me a cup of coffee in the break room, and Zales the Brilliant called us in ten.

When we walked in, one screen showed a face shot of Payton on her slab.

"You want to know what the female driver looked like to me?" Zales asked as he worked a few keys and put sunglasses on Payton. "She looked like the deceased wearing makeup and a wig."

He flashed the uneven composite on the screen, and I know my jaw dropped. The cousin. "Giselle?"

Werner straightened. "What did the male driver look like?"

"He was as evasive inside the morgue, bending over the body and scratching his ear if forced into a camera angle. But I called the ME. She said he was broad-shouldered and a bit of a know-it-all with brownish-red hair."

I looked at Werner.

"Rickard," we said together.

"We're only guessing," I pointed out. "But it could very well have been York's loyal campaign manager and York's missing daughter."

"Zales, put those videos in the York file, please, and get a crime detail to go over the morgue, inside and out. Mr. Perfect Candidate may not be such a great judge of character, after all."

Thirty-one

You can think you've made it and yet the next day's press will always be waiting for you, the public will always ask more of you. In short, you can always do better!

—GIORGIO ARMANI

Had we found Giselle? Was she the driver's intern? Or had Isobel left my father's house for a command performance?

I went into the hall and called my brother, Alex, Nick's FBI partner.

"What time did Kelsey wake up this morning?"

"About five. Why?"

"So you've been up awhile?"

"Yeah, I let Tricia sleep in for this one day before I leave for the conference. You know that. Why?"

"What time did Isobel come down to breakfast, and has she been there at the house the whole time?"

"Sixish, and absolutely yes. You saw her. Nick won't even let her go to work until you call to say you're on your way to the shop. He plans to drive her over to Vintage Magic and spend the day, by the way. I'm surprised she got to shower alone."

"No go, little brother. Stop trying to make me jealous. It won't work."

"It was worth a try. Honestly, she's been here all along. Nick, he's hardly paying attention to her, except to make sure she's safe. He's brooding over you, is what he's doing. I know my partner."

"Guilt won't work, either." Brothers, I thought. "I gotta go solve a case, but will you let Nick and Isobel know that I should be at the shop in about a half hour or so?" Alex agreed to pass along the message, and I hung up.

I followed Werner to York campaign headquarters, since it was on the way to my shop.

Ruben Rickard wasn't there, hadn't shown up today at all. Very unusual. Werner gave his hotel room a cursory look-see from the hallway. Before we left, he taped the room off and called for a search warrant and then for a neighboring town's crime scene team, since his team was still at the morgue.

He also made a conference call, including Nick, to the FBI in Boston. Afterward, he put an arm around my shoulder and walked me to my car. "The Feds are sending a couple teams to Kingston's Vineyard, one to search Rickard's house, in case he kidnapped Giselle and forced her to do his dirty work."

"She did seem rather stiff in those pictures, like she was working against her will. You think she glanced in the mirror on purpose?"

He gave me a double take. "I'll follow up that possibility. Nick's staying close to Isobel, per the Bureau, because in doing so, he can stay close to Quincy York without arousing suspicion."

"Makes sense," I said.

"Meanwhile, the Feds are also going to visit the Kingston York estate. See if Grand-mère or her henchmen are holding the missing twin against her will."

"That's the only way you could get the FBI to help, hey? Kidnapping across state lines?"

"One, it applies, and certain wording helps. Two, between Nick and I, we've got enough friends in the Bureau who listen to us. And three, we told them that solving our case might solve the York embezzling case."

"Where do we go from here?" I asked.

"We each go to our respective places of employment. You distract me." He rubbed his forehead as if he had a headache. "I can't believe we lost a body on my watch."

"You're blaming me?"

"Not at all." He opened my Element door, helped me inside, and closed it. "I'm blaming myself. I'm gonna call Nick and tell him that he has to be your bodyguard today as well as Isobel's."

"I feel rather discarded."

"You're fishing for a compliment," he said. "You're

wanted, but this isn't the time or the place. Besides, you're not ready, kiddo. You told me so."

"And you are ready?"

He leaned in and kissed me. "Oh yeah."

Scrap. "Can I call you if I have ideas about the case?"

"I'm looking forward to it. Now go before I change my mind about being a gentleman."

He watched me drive away, and I watched him in my rearview mirror until I got to the corner, all the while thinking I had to let him go. I didn't want to hurt him. I didn't want to hurt either of them.

I pulled into the Vintage Magic parking lot beside Nick's Hummer, and Isobel came out to meet me, with the contagious enthusiasm I'd come to appreciate. She handed me a Frappuccino. "Nick bought it for you, and I fitted two people. Now I'm ready to begin the alterations, but I didn't want to start, in case you had special instructions."

"I like initiative in an intern," I said, pushing my car key's lock button. *Bleep.*

Nick waited in my doorway and slapped a notebook into my hand. "Werner called an ambulance for you last night?" he'd written, the scratch marks of a couple broken pencil points visible in the text. Oy.

"I thought you were here playing all evening," he'd added.

"Not," I said, raising the Frappuccino in thanks and then taking a quick, cooling sip.

He shoved another note under my nose: "You never said they wanted to take you to the hospital."

"I take it *Tunney's* been here?"

"Nick's mad at himself because he judged you incorrectly," Isobel said.

Nick snapped his gaze her way, his expression saying, "I can speak for myself!" Which he couldn't.

Isobel shrugged. "Well, neither of you is saying how you *really* feel."

"Nick?" I asked. "When is that jaw wire coming off?"

"Now!" he wrote, a piece of pencil lead flying. He tossed the notebook and missed my trash can on his way out to the Hummer.

"You can't leave," I called. "You're Isobel's bodyguard."

He came back, grabbed Isobel's hand, and dragged her to his truck.

"Guess I'll be back," Isobel called on a chuckle, grinning as he practically pushed her into the passenger side. She stuck her head out the widow as he pulled out of my lot. "He really cares for you," she yelled, and Nick burned rubber.

Thirty-two

Almost every man looks more so in a belted trench coat.
—SYDNEY J. HARRIS

"Eve," I said, a half hour later. "You look gorgeous; your style is emerging as gothic with a steampunk edge. I love designing for you."

She posed in her fifties booties and the clockwork pinstriped jumpsuit, rust and black, that I made her. "Your idea for black cameos as part of the copper buttons was brilliant," she said.

"You have so embraced this style; I could do nothing less than give you the benefit of my design expertise. The purple hair with the rust lock up front is a good touch."

"Thanks. Kyle likes my style, too."

"Where is he?"

"He made a quick business trip back to New York for the day, so I came to play with you."

I whimpered. "I so don't have time to play with only a day and a half to Brandy's fund-raiser."

Eve pouted. "You played with Werner last night."

"You saw the paper, I take it?"

"That and I heard Tunney's story about how cozy you looked."

Good thing she hadn't talked to Stevens.

"We did get cozy. We danced to fifties tunes."

Eve about fell off her high-heeled boots. She grabbed the counter and sat on the stool behind it. "Hope is giving me heart palpitations. You're attracted to Werner."

"But I miss Nick."

Eve snorted. "Does Werner know how committed you are to him?"

"Very funny. I've tried to be honest. Which hasn't kept him from wanting more, and that worries me."

"Tell me more."

"Can't. Gotta do alterations, and my intern stepped out with Nick. Work the counter for me, like a good goth, so I can go upstairs and fix fifties outfits for Saturday."

"Since it's Thursday, I get your drift. Go, hurry." She shooed me away like a pesky fly.

I hadn't been upstairs in my sewing corner for more than two outfits when Werner came up the stairs. Sure, I liked seeing him, because I wanted to hear the latest on the case. "Do you have anything juicy to tell me? Have you caught Rickard yet? I'm betting *he's* our killer."

Werner looked good in a trench coat, and he played the handsome, silent type to perfection.

"I shouldn't let you distract me," I said getting up to meet him in the center of my mostly empty second floor, except for the caskets and horse-drawn hearses, remnants of my building's first life as the Underhill Funeral Chapel carriage house.

When I got to Werner, he reached for my face with both hands, tilted it, and fit his lips to mine.

My legs turned to jelly, but he held me up, close and tight.

When we came up for air, he didn't let me go. "I needed that," he said, smoothing my lips with a finger. "I needed you."

Oh Lordy, after a kiss like that, what did I remember but Nick's kisses? This had to stop, I was driving two good men to distraction, and it wasn't fair.

"We did get Rickard," he said, "but not the way you mean."

"I don't get it, but then I'm having trouble understanding myself right now."

Werner winked, misunderstanding me, and maybe that was best for the moment. "We found the hearse," he said, "that picked up Payton's body abandoned behind a small crematorium in Rhode Island. Rickard was inside. He's dead. He has a single needle mark that matches Payton's."

I stepped back. "Our best suspect is dead? I suppose

he can't have killed Payton, then. Does that make Giselle our killer? What's her motive?"

He shrugged. "She seems to have *greed* down to a science with all those homes, yet she could be dead, somewhere, too. And you haven't heard the worst of it."

"What could be worse than losing our prime suspect?"

"Payton was cremated with a set of forged papers as good as the ones they used to pick her up."

"I need to sit," I said, a bit sick to my stomach.

He walked me over to my sewing area, and we both took a chair. "Why cremate the body? We knew it was murder."

"But we don't know who murdered her or what was in that syringe, which is why she was going to a more comprehensive forensics lab," Werner said. "We only suspected Rickard; now he's dead, too. And what do you think Quincy York is going to say to his niece being cremated without permission from her next of kin? News at eleven?"

"So we'll never know?" I asked.

"Square one, Mad. We have to start from square one."

"You must have some evidence from the autopsy?"

He unbuttoned his coat and threw it over my workbench. "I do, actually, but I'm not sure what to do with it. It's a rare blood type."

"Rewind, please?"

"When I finished with the financials, I looked over

our suspects' and our victim's medical records. The twins and Payton shared the same rare blood type."

"No surprise. Mothers were twins, fathers are brothers."

"Only two other suspects have the same blood type."

"The candidate and the embezzler?" I guessed. "The girls' fathers? Nah, that would be too easy, wouldn't it?"

"'Fraid you're right. Grand-mère has their blood type . . . and so does Ruben Rickard."

"Hel-lo. Did you ask the old lady how he's related?"

"Sure I did. She's here in Mystic, by the way. She's staying over at the Pearl Seahorse with her son and his entourage. She says Ruben Rickard isn't related."

As a carhop call girl, she'd been carrying a baby and had chosen Slick, the wealthy, as its father. How would a kid feel if he'd been sold, even for big bucks? But I was reaching, drawing my own conclusions. "So," I said, "are you going to research Rickard's adoption?"

"You pull that out of the air?"

"Logical conclusion. So how rare is their blood? Do Rickard's parents have the same type? And are they his natural parents?"

"Evidently, half the people on Kingston's Vineyard have that blood type."

"Right, old Kingston's thirty-two children settled there. Sounds like a good place to start looking into Rickard's family tree."

"You astound me," Werner said. "You get right to the root of the problem. Zip, no forethought."

If only he knew. "I spent my life getting into trouble for speaking without thinking. My father hates it. Now, you commend me for it. Maybe that's why I like you so much."

"I sure hope it's more than that."

Oh, bad timing to answer that, even if I was sure of the answer, which I wasn't.

"Have you told Quincy York yet that his niece has been cremated without her father's permission?"

"I stopped here first for moral support, and maybe a kiss? Quincy's gonna call another press conference, and I'll rightly be raked over the coals for losing his niece's body and letting her get cremated."

"It's called a crime, which you *didn't* commit. Werner, skip the candidate. Go see his brother, Patrick. Tell him what happened to his daughter. See if he'll sign off or give permission after the fact. He seems like a man who would empathize with the need for forgiveness."

"You're right. Patrick needs to know, not Quincy."

"Right," I said. "The candidate should look to his own family. He loses track of them, then he's surprised bad things happen."

"Bad things?"

"Like his wife's plane crash. That was horrific. I wonder if Rickard had anything to do with that."

Werner froze. "Are you a conspiracy theorist?"

"Not especially, but when you talk to Grand-mère, try asking her what happened to her husband."

"Because?"

"Nobody talks about him. Ever. Like he never existed."

"Mad, you're making me crazy with theories that don't have anything to do with Payton's murder."

In for a penny. "Did you investigate Madame Robear? It still bothers me that the owner of a modeling agency initially identified Payton as Isobel. It's just so odd that she would get the identification wrong." Because even though Isobel modeled for her, I think Giselle worked for her as a call girl.

"I tried to contact Robear," Werner said. "She's put her modeling agency in the hands of an assistant and skipped the country. She left no forwarding address."

"I worked with her models in New York, you know? She might once have mentioned an Anatole Sevigny from France." She might, though she hadn't. "She could be at his place as we speak, Château Sevigny. Call him; ask him about Madame Celine Robear."

"You're sure honing your sleuthing skills, Mad. Are you bucking for my job?"

"Nope, I'm bucking to clear Isobel's name and put her family in jail, if they're guilty, which I think they are. As sin."

"I think you're right," Nick said, stepping into the light, his hand on his sore jaw.

"How does it feel?" I asked.

"It hurts, but I'm glad I can talk again. Isobel said I'm supposed to be your bodyguard now, too?"

Werner cleared his throat. "Give her up, already."

"It'll never happen," Nick said as he went downstairs.

Thirty-three

A designer can mull over complicated designs for months.
Then suddenly the simple, elegant, beautiful solution occurs
to him. When it happens to you, it feels as if God is talking!
And maybe He is. —LEO FRANKOWSKI

Go home, Detective, Nick said a half hour later, checking his watch as we all admired Isobel's skill while she
did her first public solo fitting.

She was a fashion professional. She knew the primo
designers by pecking order, she aced style, knew the
lingo, fashion gossip, and how to do a difficult fitting
while complimenting a customer with both the outfit
and the right words.

I looked forward to seeing her altering skills, but I
was already certain she was the right York for me, the
model who went to fashion school.

Brandy had actually found me a great intern, albeit
with a wacked-out family.

What I saw was what I got: Isobel York in the flesh,

too blatantly honest—annoyingly so, sometimes—to be her own twin. Much too spontaneously indiscreet to be a call girl. And she couldn't be submissive if her life depended on it.

Meanwhile, Nick had been doing some disgruntled pacing since Werner told him to let me go. "Detective, isn't it time you went back to the station?" Nick suggested.

Eve chuckled at seeing Nick thwarted. "Jaconetti," Eve said. "I always said you took Mad for granted. Seven years she lived in New York, and you visited like three times."

Nick ran a hand through his hair. "I was on assignment."

"Interminably? You knew she'd be there waiting, whenever. Now maybe she won't be."

I turned to Nick. "I'm doing some private sleuthing on Payton's case. No need to worry about me."

Nick scoffed. "You mean the detective doesn't mind, for the first time ever, that you're sleuthing? That doesn't tip you off to his intentions?"

"We're collaborating."

Werner gave Nick a cocky grin. "Yes, we are."

"According to Mystick Falls gossip," Eve said, examining her copper fingernails, "Werner's *attentions* tip Mad off to his intentions."

"Eve!" I snapped.

Dante, my ghost, who loved gatherings this size, chuckled and winked.

"Sorry, Mad, but it's out," Eve said. "You two have been seen all over town, sometimes standing a bit close, sometimes with a bit of lip action. Tunney or the Sweets could give you a list of times, locations, and the corresponding body moves."

Isobel walked her interested customer to the door while I thanked the stars that my phone rang. I answered and let Nick cool off a bit.

"Good news," I said, hanging up. "The MacKenzie Carousel is being set up at Cort's now. Rory and Vickie MacKenzie are there. They're not charging her for this stop on their tour, and they've made a big donation to the Nurture Kids Foundation."

"That's wonderful," Isobel said, returning from seeing her customer out. "Are we going to be able to close Vintage Magic to attend?"

"It's my sister Brandy's event. We sure are." I looked around the shop to make sure my pregnant sister didn't walk in. "We're also closing on Sunday for my sister Sherry's baby shower."

Isobel clapped her hands. "What's the itinerary for Saturday?"

There's a garden party–style vintage car show in the afternoon, with models wearing fifties designer clothes to show off the cars. That's when you can ride the carousel Rory's ancestor carved that Rory maintains."

"I can't wait," Isobel said. "I wouldn't miss this for

anything. What does it cost to get in? I mean there has to be a charge if it's a fund-raiser."

"It's five hundred dollars a ticket," I said, "but I'll need you there. You're hired for the day, so no cost to you."

"Grand-mère probably won't like that. Bet she'll pay for my ticket. She's a pushover for anything that supports kids without parents."

I'll bet. "I'd like to meet Grand-mère."

"Maybe my whole family can come? The Yorks are rich enough, and maybe it'll get Daddy's attention away from the campaign for a bit. He might actually *see* me."

"I hope your dad looks good in a tux, because in the evening there's a bachelor auction, and he's agreed to be auctioned off." I knew he'd do anything for publicity, which is why I wasn't afraid to ask. "I'll bet your father will bring a pretty penny. Nick and Werner here will be up for bid, too."

They groaned, suddenly on equal ground.

"Who are you gonna bid on, Mad?" Isobel asked, looking at Nick and Werner as if she'd take the one I didn't want.

"I don't plan to bid, thanks. Right now, I'm off to the Vancortland estate. Coming, Eve? Isobel, can you and Nick lock up?"

Isobel slipped her arm through Nick's. "Will do, boss."

"Werner, guess it's back to the station for you." Nick sounded hopeful.

"Werner might want to come with us and talk to Brandy," I suggested. "She got mugged that fateful day, which is what kept her from meeting Isobel on the train. Brandy might have been able to tell that Isobel wasn't herself—she was Payton. And, Werner, Brandy might have *seen* her own mugger."

"I got robbed, too," Isobel said, not to be outdone. "They took my ticket and used it for Payton."

Werner frowned. "I can't imagine why they wouldn't buy fresh tickets."

"I believe the point was to keep Brandy and Isobel *off* the train," I said. "They might have gotten in the way of the switch. The murderers might also have wanted to confuse the world about which cousin was which, like in the shell game," I added. "Move the walnut shells around and guess which one has the pea beneath it. Maybe someone's using the family to toy with Candidate York in a very big way, but he's too self-absorbed to notice. Sorry, Isobel, I know he's your father."

Isobel made a wry face. "It's okay; he stepped off the family radar when my mother passed, except for Grand-mère, of course, who pulls his strings. But this is all like that wake-up call, isn't it?" She shivered.

Werner turned to face her. "Why do you say it in that tone?"

"I got a second voice-modulated call. The caller said I should be dead, like Payton, and that my dad was in for a wake-up call."

"When?" Werner snapped. "Why didn't you tell us? I thought we had a trace on this phone."

"No, they called me at Mr. Cutler's house. I'm sorry, it seemed like more of the same, and since I have Nick guarding me. . . . Listen, being self-absorbed is a family trait I've been trying to kick."

"Nick, stick to her like glue," Werner said. "Mad, you go ask Brandy the right questions for me." He checked his watch. "I need to see Patrick York. Then Quincy. I'm going to spell out the dangers to the candidate's family and make him understand, if I have to rub his nose in it."

"Go, Mad," Eve said.

"Thanks, let's go." I gave a general wave. "See you later."

"Will you?" Werner asked. "My house, later?"

"To discuss the case? Sure. Nick, Isobel, join us? You have as much to add as I do. Werner, want me to bring something?"

Eve scoffed. "Yeah, he wanted you to bring a toothbrush, doof, not a posse."

Nick gave a half nod. "What time?"

Thirty-four

Fashion is the science of appearance, and it inspires one with
the desire to seem rather than to be. —HENRY FIELDING

"Detective Werner," Isobel said, coming into Vintage
Magic on the morning of the fund-raiser. "I don't know
what you said to my father, but he hugged me really tight
this morning, like he meant it." Her eyes filled. "Thanks."

I squeezed Isobel's shoulder as I passed her to hang the
two outfits yet to be picked up at the front. "The minute you
get these out the door, you and Nick head over to Vancortland House. I'll need you to help dress the models."

"I'd like that," Nick said.

"Not you, Jaconetti," Eve said. "Your thing is *un-
dressing* women."

I ignored them both. "At noon, whether those outfits
have been picked up or not, close Vintage Magic and
come to Cort's. Stay with her, Nick."

He saluted. "That's my job, right, watching Isobel's body?"

"It sure is. And, Eve, you're coming with me, now."

"I'm your right-hand goth for the day. Kyle's already at Cort's, probably putting a polish on his Lamborghini and drooling over the other vintage cars."

I set five comped Carousel of Love tickets on the counter. "These are for any of you who find the five-hundred-dollar entry fee a burden. You've been a big help to me, to my sister Brandy, and by extension, to the Nurture Kids Foundation; it's the least we can do."

Werner walked me to my car. "I won't be there until later, kiddo. There's still a killer on the loose."

"Sorry we couldn't get together last night after all. Are you closing in?"

"I hope so," he said. "The FBI says that Rickard was living with a woman on Kingston's Vineyard. We don't know who yet, but I'm betting it was Giselle. They sent me some paperwork right before I left the station to come here, and I've yet to go over it."

Giselle and Rickard? Yuck. "Do you have a picture of Rickard in the files at the station?"

"I have the file in my car. Why?"

"May I see it?"

Call it a hunch, but I needed to see Rickard from the back. "Something about him caught my attention the day he identified Payton. I'd just like another look."

Werner brought me the file, and flipping through,

looking for the photos, I spotted a canceled check for twenty-five grand, but I couldn't make out the signature. When I moved it, I noticed that it was clipped to paperwork from Rhode Island social services. Ruben Rickard did not grow up in wealth, but in a series of foster homes.

I didn't linger on the document but found the pictures of his corpse, looked at and discarded one after another, until I found what I wanted. The back of Rickard's head. That's why he spooked me; he could very well be Gian, the boat client. The man Giselle or Payton was so shocked to see.

No, I didn't have proof as to which cousin was the present-day call girl, I reminded myself, just a lot of nebulous evidence, however inadmissible.

"You can't afford this," the York call girl had said. "Are you skimming from the top?" Like . . . skimming from the candidate's campaign contributions, maybe?

If Giselle *had* been the call girl, I wondered if, rather than blackmailing each other, they decided to join forces.

No, I still doubted whether Rickard and the call girl could be living or working/killing together. He had skeeved the Hermès out of her on that boat. It didn't make sense.

Worse, if my wild assumptions were correct, Rickard was an uncle to the cousins. Yuck. And if I was right about that, I sure hoped they knew it. Problem: I learned the nauseating facts in a vision and couldn't tell a soul. Except Nick, and—

Wait a minute, maybe I could plumb Grand-mère's memories.

"Madeira Cutler," Werner said. "Your mind's working a mile a minute."

I looked up at him. "Is it?"

"I can practically see the gears turning. Any conclusions?"

"You'll be the first to know."

"See you at Vancortland's, later," he said watching my lips, but he stepped back. "Tonight, may I have the first dance? If I'm there on time."

I nodded. "Thank you for asking." I watched him pull out of my lot and turn onto Main. Then I went back in the shop. "Isobel, you're bringing everything we found in Grand-mère's trunk, skates and all, right?"

"Just like you said, boss."

"Nick, she'll need your help to hang the clothes . . . in the Element, because they need clothes racks, darn it." I got out my keys and rolled my eyes. "I'll drive the Hummer."

We traded keys, and Nick followed me to Little Black Dress Lane, where I found an Anne Fogarty long-sleeved black jersey dress. I also stopped at Mad as a Hatter for a black straw hat with a face veil.

"You going as a woman in mourning?" he asked.

"Au contraire. I'll explain later. Stop by my dad's and get a shovel, will you? A big-ascot ditch digger. Oh, and a couple fake gravestones from our Halloween display."

"Do you have a fever?" he asked, hand to my brow.

"No, sort of. Just don't forget, you're my go-to guy."

"Feels good to hear you say so."

Isobel followed us outside.

"Find me when you get to Cort's, please. I'll have assignments for both of you."

"Will do, boss."

Nick saluted again, then from the doorway, he watched me, as did Dante, wagging a "You be careful" finger at me from beside Nick.

The Hummer rumbled to life with a loud belch, as would any machine or human that ran on aged French fry oil.

I smiled, wishing I could enter the camouflaged beast in the car show. I patted the steering wheel. "Bet you'd win best in class, Junebug."

Thirty-five

The fifties and sixties were a time of innocence and innocence destroyed. Fashion ruled the day, separating the "squares" from the "cool," the "Ivy League" from those that would later come to be labeled "Radicals." —ANGELA EPPS

Nick and Isobel arrived at Cort's at eleven, after the last two outfits were picked up.

Vintage cars had been placed strategically around the grounds, some along the front of Cort's carriage house, some inside, but I'd requested three bright, big-finned beauties in pastel colors—turquoise, pink, and mint green—to be placed along the circular drive.

"Isobel, I found that most of Robear's models can roller-skate. Three are waiting for the carhop uniforms. Run them inside, will you?"

Isobel grabbed the uniforms. "Is Madame Robear here?" she asked.

"No, I forgot to tell you she was unable to attend, but

her assistant's running the show. You must have worked with Angela when you worked for Robear."

"I did. I'll say hello."

"Nick, Eve will show you inside where to put the other clothes from the Element's racks. We've already picked the models and given them their instructions. When you're done, come back for your instructions. We open the gates in less than an hour."

I breathed a sigh of relief when the models dressed in fifties outfits were finally costumed and beside the vintage cars assigned to them. Also set to roll were the carhops, who'd skate to and from the cars and around the circular drive, fake trays raised high.

That scenario inspired me to have fifties music piped outside, done in a flash, compliments of Sherry's husband, Justin, Cort's son, who grew up in the house.

A short while later, in character, I wore a red, wide-notch-collar sheath dress, its skirt slit to my thigh, long red button-gloves, a black and red half hat with a black veil, and my trusty red Louboutin follow-me pumps.

Early on, I greeted Vickie and Rory MacKenzie and Vickie's half sisters, identical triplets, Harmony, Destiny, and Storm, and their hunky husbands. Melody Seabright brought her husband, Logan, and Kira Fitzgerald Goddard brought her husband, Jason.

Kira gave Brandy some great tips on running a bachelor auction. And I took Vickie up on her offer of an antique carousel ride.

Afterward, I wished I could continue to play and enjoy. Instead, I fidgeted on Cort's marble steps and checked my jeweled watch pin every other minute. "The gates are about to open," I said over my walkie-talkie. "Isobel, will you stay out front here and watch for your family? And when they arrive, introduce your dad to Brandy and Cort and then bring Grand-mère to me. Do you mind?"

"Anything you say, boss. I'll go watch for them near the gate."

Sometimes I wasn't sure if her calling me boss was compliment or condescension, but she did seem to enjoy working for me.

I let Nick in on my vision-inspired plan and asked him to play a small role in the gambit.

Grand-mère arrived early, chauffeured in that powder blue stretch limo, only ten years too new to join in the day's vintage car competition.

Isobel brought Grand-mère first to Brandy and Cort. I approved her startled reaction to the carhops. Step one, catch her off guard.

Isobel then put Grand-mère into my capable hands and went to take Nick's arm. They would stroll, seemingly at random, about fifty or sixty feet behind us, not always in viewing range.

"Bette," I said, holding Grand-mère's arm for a stroll. "Or is it Lizzie or Betsy?"

She gave me a double take.

"Isobel says you go by lots of names."

"Oh, yes, Elizabeth has so many nicknames."

"You were checking up on your granddaughter at my shop the day she was supposed to arrive, weren't you?"

"Vintage Magic is a lovely shop," she said.

The Sweets must have recognized Grand-mère from that first day, because they waved and came for a chat. I kept checking my watch. If they delayed us much longer, they'd ruin my plan.

I think Ethel caught on because she gave me a wink and urged Dolly toward the refreshment tent.

"Where were we?" Grand-mère asked. "Oh, your little shop. It's almost good enough for my Isobel. I was skeptical, but she loves her work and her new boss."

"Glad to hear it. So what do you think of Vancortland House? We in Mystick Falls are quite proud of it."

"Your brother-in-law owns it, is that right?"

"No, the owner is my sister Sherry's father-in-law."

I walked Grand-mère by the carhops and felt her body stiffen while her pulse picked up speed. "Thanks for that trunk of wonderful clothes, and those carhop uniforms. Those must have been the days, working around all that energy. Great music, awesome tips; you must have felt free as a bird skating for a living."

"No one is ever free, young lady," she snapped.

I walked her beside the carousel, so she could calm down while she admired it, then we crossed the lawn, passing a display of vintage cars, and the judges ranking them, on our way to Cort's carriage house.

When the side door of the carriage house flew unexpectedly open and slammed against the building, Grandmère jumped.

Eve stepped out, wearing Grand-mère's yellow sleeveless boatneck dress with the embroidered bands, carrying my niece, Kelsey.

Nick went up to her and demanded "the child."

"Twenty-five grand," Eve said, holding out her hand.

Nick slapped a fake check into it. Eve gave him the baby, went back into the carriage house, and Nick walked away.

The tableau might never have taken place.

Nevertheless, Grand-mère stood frozen. "Twen—" She cleared her throat. "Twenty-five thousand dollars?" Her voice quavered.

"What?" I asked.

Her gaze snapped up to mine, her expression haunted. "Nothing."

I patted her hand. "Care for a flask of whiskey?"

"Beg pardon?"

"A glass of punch," I said. "Are you thirsty?"

"No thank you." Sweat had formed on her upper lip.

Eventually, we passed a tree with two fake gravestones beneath it. On the opposite side, revealed as we passed, stood a woman wearing a long-sleeved black swirl dress, hat veil over her face, head averted, leaning on a shovel.

Grand-mère stumbled, but I helped her catch her balance. She fumbled in her purse for a handkerchief, thank the stars, and when she looked back, the model and the gravestones had disappeared.

"Isobel told me about her grandfather." *Beat, beat, beat.* "Imagine disappearing like that . . ." *beat* ". . . as if in a puff of smoke, never to be heard from again."

Grand-mère looked daggers at me, not a little frightening. That deadly focus hadn't ended well the last time.

I fluffed my hair, the sign for help. I couldn't take a chance that she still carried a revolver all these years later. She looked that wild-eyed.

Nick and Isobel stepped up beside us, the old lady trembling visibly.

Isobel took her grandmother's purse and clutched it to her chest.

We watched Nick escort Grand-mère back toward the house. It looked like he got her talking, and once he did, she didn't seem to want to stop.

Nick would call Werner if she confessed, which I deeply hoped she would. I was almost sorry I'd spooked her so badly. But, well, several people had died, now. If not for Ruben Rickard, her illegitimate son—if my guess was correct—her legitimate granddaughter, Payton, might still be alive.

"Boss," Isobel said, "that little show you set up

spooked the hell out of my grandmother. What do you know that I don't?"

I squeezed Isobel's opposite shoulder in a half hug. "Well, sweetie, that's the sad part. I don't *know* a thing. Only Grand-mère does, and she may never tell."

Thirty-six

A dress makes no sense unless it inspires men to want to take it off you.
—FRANÇOISE SAGAN

It had been an afternoon filled with pointy bras, poodle skirts, off-the-shoulder sweaters, roller skates, and carousel rides.

The evening was another story.

My outfit consisted of a long black lace evening gown over cream satin, figure-hugging, V-neck, strapless.

The orchestra played through dinner and after.

I had danced the first dance with Nick, gorgeous in an Armani tux, and not a bad dancer, even to "The Yellow Rose of Texas."

Werner, yummy in his tux, arrived in time to claim me for a later dance, the "Tennessee Waltz."

"Sorry I missed dinner. Late break in the case." His hand at my back hesitated when he found bare skin.

Then he skimmed the entire area to the exposed base of my spine before he worked his way back up, as if memorizing the shape of it with the tips of his fingers.

"If I have a heart attack," he whispered, "you'll hold me up, right?"

I stepped back to look at him. "Why would you do that?"

"You're wearing black lace stenciled on bare skin. Kinda hard on a man. Good thing *you're* not up for bid."

"Would I bring a pretty penny?"

"You don't need to fish for compliments, just wipe the drool off my chin now and again, so no one else sees it, 'kay?"

He twirled me fast and unexpectedly, and I laughed.

"I hate to ruin this moment with shop talk," he said against my ear, "but I need to take my mind off you beneath that dress. The old lady, Grand-mère, the candidate's mother; she shed a lot of light on the case, today. Nick called for backup and met us outside the gates with her so as not to cause a scene."

"Really?" I actually hadn't known that. "Tell me what happened."

"You won't believe it. At first she was confused, talked about seeing things. Then she said since Payton had been killed she thought that maybe a few things needed to be cleared up. I get the impression that something you did reminded her of her obligation in that regards, but I'm not clear on that. And neither was she."

I shrugged. "What did she say?"

"She told me that she gave birth to a third son, but her husband was a good-for-nothing drunk. She couldn't afford another mouth to feed, so she sold it to a rich Newport family for twenty-five grand. Not a good way to make a buck, not legal either, but she fed her two boys for a long time, she said, and she invested wisely and grew her nest egg to its present size."

"That explains the canceled check in the file the Feds found in Rickard's house," I said. "He must have had to do some deep and dirty investigating to get his hands on that."

"That's exactly what it was, and yes, some breaking and entering in his background might have played into his investigation of his roots, because it was originally supposed to be a closed adoption. Looks like the candidate's brother killed his own niece," Werner murmured. "Explains the rare blood type match, though."

"Sure does."

"Anyway," he said, "according to the records, the family she sold him to never did adopt him. He's listed as being a problem child, prone to losing his temper and assaulting other children."

"I don't believe he changed much," I said, "and he only added fury and resentment of his biological family to his list of grievances with the world."

"The people who 'bought' him gave Rickard to social services as a toddler. I agree that Rickard's motive was probably a long-held grudge over being sold. But why kill Payton, the poor embezzler's daughter. Why not the favorite twin, the rich one? Make a profit?"

"Which one's the favorite?" I asked. "In your opinion."

"Personally, I think it should be your intern, but she thinks her twin's the favorite."

"Yeah, Isobel does think Giselle is the favorite. So what did the old lady do with her drunk husband, divorce him?"

"No, that's the sad part. He came after her with a broken bottle in a drunken rage one night, and she shot him. Killed him in self-defense. She even told us where she buried him."

"Wow, so, no arrest, then?"

"Not yet, but she's already on the psych ward at the Mystick Falls Hospital for evaluation. We thought we'd tell her son tomorrow. They're not that close, and no need to ruin Brandy's night."

"Why a psych eval?" I asked, looking for his tip-off.

"Ah, she said it all happened again today. That's what made her step forward. She saw a baby being sold for twenty-five grand, a dozen brazen carhops, a woman with a shovel at the cemetery; they were signs, she said. That's when she knew she had to clear her conscience."

And a dandy job she did. Not. No mention of carhopping or bed-hopping or of shooting hubby in cold blood. She'd come out squeaky clean, except for burying the old man on her own. On the other hand, after all these years, she might have come to believe in her own innocence.

"What have we got for loose ends now?" I asked.

"What? Sorry, I'm distracted by your naked waist beneath this thing."

"Well, get your hand out of there. There's nothing to find. This is the kind of dress you want against your bare skin."

"You had to tell me that?"

"Talk to me. We don't know why Payton or Rickard are dead. And we haven't found Giselle."

"Way to throw cold water on a guy."

"You asked for it." I sighed and rested my head on his shoulder.

"What's bothering you, kiddo?" Werner asked. "Not that I don't love having you this close."

"Payton's cremation's bothering me. Why would Giselle go so far as to cremate her cousin, even if she did kill her? Why not let the family bury her?"

"Rickard might have done it," Werner said. "Partners in crime often have partings of the way. Maybe he and Giselle broke up."

"Yeah, well, they were uncle and niece, so one would hope so."

"Broke up the gang, I mean," Werner said. "The gang. Let's assume he had enough ethics to treat Giselle like a niece."

"Anyway, that's not it," I said, biting the inside of my lip for a minute. "It's . . . the obliteration. No way to look back. Makes me think there was something else to hide."

The music stopped, Brandy took the microphone, and we sat down. She gave a formal welcome from the Nurture Kids Foundation and told us a bit about the cause with a PowerPoint presentation going on behind her. Just enough show-and-tell to make us open our purses . . . for tissues and checkbooks.

After her individual and profuse thanks, my sister invited the bachelors up for bid to gather in the room off the ballroom. Werner, Nick, Kyle, Cort, Candidate York, and my dad, among others, left looking like they were going to their own hangings.

We were all women now at our table, and we had a good laugh over their plight, most planning on winning their own men.

Except for Isobel and me. The two of us decided, between us, to mix it up a bit—mix up the couples, I mean. Have some fun.

Thirty-seven

Fashion anticipates, and elegance is a state of mind . . . a mirror of the time in which we live, a translation of the future, and should never be static. —OLEG CASSINI

Sherry's husband, Justin, as master of ceremonies, brought out Dolly Sweet on a wheeled stool and set her before the mike on the opposite side of the stage from him, to introduce the bachelors. She wore the Katharine Hepburn gown I'd given her, and she looked grand.

A brilliant and inspired choice, Dolly could be as bawdy as she wanted, and everyone would be charmed.

Dolly gave a signal to dim the applause and eyed my brother-in-law. "I know you belong to Sherry, cupcake, but you'll make sure I don't roll off the stage, won't you, sweet thing?"

Justin bowed her way. "Cupcake on duty."

Dolly picked up her notes. "Our bidding starts this evening with the one and only Justin Vancortland IV, our generous and hunky host for the evening, and the father of cupcake, over here. Let's give our benefactor a rousing round of applause."

We gave Cort a standing ovation, while Brandy slipped into a seat at our table.

"Ready for the bidding, Sis?" I asked her.

She grabbed my hand on one side and Sherry's on the other. "I've never been so nervous in my life. I don't even know if he wants me to bid on him."

"Sure you do," I said. "I saw the way he looked at you while you were dancing."

Brandy grinned, a rare and wonderful sight.

Isobel escorted Cort onstage—that was her task for the evening, bachelor escort—and Dolly read Cort's bio. "When not overseeing his railroad companies, Cort can be found proudly escorting his granddaughter Vanessa around town. Oh, and he wanted me to say he can't wait to install that second baby seat in his car."

Dolly chuckled. "You're my kind of man, Cort. For his auction date, ladies, Cort will take you for a leisurely sail on the Mystic River, where you'll share an intimate gourmet dinner at sunset."

Justin V, Sherry's husband, gave his podium over to a professional auctioneer.

Dolly raised her paddle. "I'd like to start the bidding on this young buck with a grand."

The bidding escalated and ended with Cort escorting Brandy offstage. He'd gone for ten grand. A good beginning for the event, and probably Brandy's life savings, but she acted like he was so worth it. It was also possible that the foundation bankrolled her to get things off to a hefty start.

My father came up for bid next. His offered date: a weekend in the Finger Lakes. Sure, everyone in Mystick Falls knew, after our parents named us Sherry, Brandy, and Madeira, that my father could get real sexy after a day at the Finger Lakes wineries.

And though Fiona should probably resent his lack of originality, she became blatantly outrageous and ferocious in her bidding. Twenty thousand dollars went to the Nurture Kids Foundation for Harry Cutler, mild-mannered English professor.

"I hope Dad doesn't stroke out," I told Sherry.

She giggled; we both did. My father was such a private, frugal man. The look on his face at Fiona's winning bid was priceless but nothing to his reaction when she kissed him right there in front of God and the gossips of Mystick Falls.

"Talk about making a claim," I said.

"Yeah, but look," Sherry said. "Dad's cooperating."

"Go, Dad!" My sisters and I whistled, yelled, applauded, and cheered.

He zoomed in on us and waved, one brow raised, a promise of retribution in his half smile.

"Well," Dolly said, "it's about damned time, Harry, with your car always in Fee's driveway."

We screamed at the double entendre, and my dad went over and bussed Dolly right on the lips.

"Well, shut my mouth," Dolly said. "Congratulations, Fiona!"

My father escorted a laughing Fiona off the stage.

A shapely female latecomer walked in and took an empty chair across the room. Somebody who liked to make an entrance or wanted to be seen by this audience in particular. Dressed to kill in what looked like it could be Armani Privé, the stunner had lush long black hair with a blue streak rippling down her back. Her thick, heavy makeup was a fashion faux pas, but her long legs looked great in those strappy Manolo Blahniks.

I was so focused on her, I failed to realize that Werner was up for bid. When I knew and still failed to bid, Eve poked me one time too many, the last time, so sharply she knocked the paddle out of my hand, grabbed it before me, raised it, and outbid a blonde for sixteen thousand five hundred dollars, winning Werner in my name.

I hadn't wanted to stoke the gossips, but there I was claiming my cop off the stage to Eve's whistles and catcalls.

"There's my Maddie," Dolly said, in case the world didn't already know, "getting her man. Nick, my boy, you gotta step it up a notch."

Eve's cheer broke the awkward silence, and I applauded to get everyone going while Werner and I made our way back to our table. Ah heck, it was worth the money to make him so happy. My former friend Eve, however, was another matter. She'd totally ruined Isobel's and my plan to mix it up. So I pulled a similar stunt when Nick came up for bid by throwing a red shawl over Eve's shoulders. You'd think it was yellow paint the way she stood and raised her arms to shrug it off, paddle in hand.

She ended up paying twenty-two grand for a man she couldn't stand. Well, for charity, and we all knew it. You wouldn't know it to look at Eve, and especially not at her frugal mother, but Mystick Falls was not an inexpensive community to live in. The Meyerses came from a long line of German toy manufacturers, and they were loaded. They simply preferred not to spend it.

Dolly started the bid at a grand for each and every man, to raise the foundation's profits, I was sure. Meanwhile, the women took to laughing or heckling her every time she raised her paddle.

"Hey, you can't want them all," one woman yelled.

"Listen, chickie," Dolly said. "I'm nearly a hundred and four, and I wanna go out smiling."

Isobel won Kyle, to Eve's dismay, so Isobel's half of the "mix it up" plan worked, and then she went back to work onstage. The world ran amok, the foundation made a profit, and Dolly had a blast.

When Candidate Quincy York finally came up for bid, the room went wild. Every woman there knew he didn't belong to anybody. This was a free-for-all, and the Nurture Kids Foundation would benefit big time.

For York, the conspicuous latecomer raised her paddle often and countered every bid. Finally she stood, and the room stilled. "One hundred thousand dollars."

Nobody applauded at first except Brandy, Justin, and Dolly, but after the shock wore off, confetti rained down from the ceiling, signaling the successful end of the auction.

The winner went onstage to claim York, and on their way offstage, she somehow hooked arms with Isobel, so the three of them disappeared together.

York had been the final bachelor, the pièce de résistance, so heck, maybe Isobel made the first move. I hadn't been watching that closely.

We ordered another round of drinks to celebrate, except for Nick and Eve, who were furious with me, Sherry who had a backache and asked Justin to take her home, and Tricia, also pregnant, who thought going home was a fine idea, so she and my brother, Alex, left as well.

When the orchestra started again, I stood to look for Isobel, and when I didn't see her, York, or his winner, panic rushed through me. I grabbed Nick's hand, then Werner's, and pulled them out of their chairs and didn't let go until they followed me on their own, at a near run across the ballroom.

Eve and Kyle got up and followed.

I looked behind the stage, we all did, but York wasn't there, and neither was Isobel or the winning bidder.

Giselle?

Thirty-eight

In order to be irreplaceable one must always be different.
—COCO CHANEL

Behind the stage, the back terrace doors stood open, so we went outside into the dark, empty night, Nick calling for backup.

Before us rolled about a half mile's worth of sloping lawns to the cliff's edge, and the Mystic River beyond, with a deadly, rocky drop to the beach.

A gun went off.

A scream echoed in the distance.

"Isobel!" I called.

Werner and Nick took off at a run across the lawn toward the water.

I gave Kyle Nick's keys. "Get the Hummer near the carriage house, and drive it down to the cliff. Headlights would be a big help."

"Ack," Eve said, "Kyle, be careful not to drive over the edge."

He chuckled and ran.

I went back to the terrace and flipped on a bank of light switches, but it wasn't nearly enough illumination to reach that far. From experience, Eve and I both knew to kick off our shoes before we started running.

It wasn't long before I saw a body and swerved toward it.

"What the hell?" Eve snapped, making a sharp left ahead of me and doubling back.

"A body," I said, kneeling beside it, but then I released my breath. "Not a body. A dress and shoes." I picked them up and continued running.

"Drop the clothes!" Eve yelled. "You'll make better time."

"I can run as fast carrying them."

"Why would you want to?"

"Armani Privé? Manolos? One of a kind? Worth more than Kyle's car."

"You can be such a fruitloop!" Eve screamed, and took the running lead.

The lights of Nick's Hummer came over the hill before the Hummer itself, and lit our way, though Kyle drove like he was drunk. Then I realized he was scanning the area with the lights.

When everything appeared clear, Kyle gunned the

Hummer across Cort's million-dollar lawn, but who cared? People's lives were in peril.

Five people went out ahead of us—Nick, Werner, York, Isobel, and the latecomer—and only one person stood at the edge of the cliff. "Oh God."

I stopped to catch my breath and lay the outfit on a wrought iron bench Cort kept down there, the Manolos on top so the gown wouldn't blow away.

"Nick," I called, "where's Werner?"

Nick was waving a flashlight. "He's gone down for Isobel."

I looked over the edge. Two young women lay at the base of the cliffs, looking like broken dolls in the sand, though they'd landed a distance away from each other. And they were both wearing black cocktail dresses, when one of them should be in her slip, or less.

The latecomer must have been wearing two layers. I couldn't tell which was which. "Oh God. Isobel, are you all right?" I shouted.

Kyle parked the car and left the headlights on.

Ambulances and police cars, no lights, no sirens, cut through Cort's neighbor's yard for easier access to a set of steps through the cliff rock to the beach.

I took Nick's tux jacket off him, stepped out of my dress behind it, and slipped into it. "Here. Hold this," I said, giving him the dress. Then I buttoned myself into his jacket and made my way down the face of the cliff.

"Good thing you're a spider monkey, fruitloop," Eve

called after me. "I'll put this dress with your stash. You'd better not fall. I'll never forgive you, if you . . ."

Her voice cracked, but I kept going.

I went to Werner, kneeling over one of the girls, the one nearest the water. The gash on her head bled profusely into the sand.

"Madeira," the girl said. "I love working for you. I hope this doesn't change anything."

Isobel never called me Madeira, ever. She called me boss so often, I was starting to get sick of it. "You're Giselle, aren't you?"

"Oh, yes. Giselle, that's the one." She touched her head. "I'm the favorite. I'm *supposed* to be the favorite. It's my turn to have all the money. Giselle lives so far away—no, I . . . *I* live so far from the family, it'll be easy to be Giselle. They won't know. They don't care." She groaned. "I have a really bad headache."

Not Giselle, I realized then, but Payton trying, and failing with her last breath, to claim Giselle's life and fortune. I looked at Werner, and he shook his head like he doubted she'd make it. I agreed.

"Where's York?" I asked him.

"On an outcropping of rock. He's been shot by Payton here, but he's moving. They're about to bring him up, see?"

I left Werner with Payton and went to Isobel. "Isobel, you okay?"

"My sister's gone, boss. Giselle is the one who died."

255

"I know that now, sweetie."

"Payton was the killer all along. Payton bid on my dad; what a joke if she'd succeeded and won him as her father, exactly as she wanted. Except that she also wanted to kill him."

"That's why she had the body *cremated*. She planned to take Giselle's place," I said.

"Yes, Payton told me as much on our way down here. She thought she should get all the money since she'd never had any of it. It was time, she said. She shot my dad when he tried to reason with her. She didn't think we'd recognize her in that getup. She said she was sorry about Giselle but only after she fell. She was bringing us to that boat. My dad and I were supposed to drown tonight. Is my dad okay?"

"It looks like he is. I can see him responding to the medics. He's moving his hands."

Isobel smiled. "He does that."

"Looks like you've been shot in the shoulder," I said.

"And my side, I think, but the shoulder hurts more."

"Medics," I called at the top of my lungs.

Werner joined me. "I got a statement, but she's gone," he said. "That was a self-inflicted wound."

Isobel wept. So did I, though I tried to comfort her.

Werner put an arm around me.

"You just left Payton, you know? She was the killer. Giselle died on the train."

"Isobel and Giselle both worked for Robear," Werner said. "Isobel as a model, Giselle as a call girl."

"What?" I didn't know he knew that.

"Robear led a double life. She was literally a madam. I talked to Sevigny in France. The French authorities forwarded his sworn statement. Did you know, Isobel, about Giselle working for Robear, too?" he asked.

"Robear tried to recruit me as a call girl when I first started modeling for her. Going by the name of Madam C., she sold high-priced models to men who could afford anything. I told Giselle because I was upset—that's when we lived together—and thought nothing more about it. I modeled, and that's all."

I dabbed at Isobel's brow with the corner of Nick's jacket.

"During the course of this investigation," Isobel continued, "after the body was identified as me, then Payton, it did make me think of how easy we could pretend to be each other. I thought of Robear's offer and Giselle's travels. But Robear had left the country by then, and I couldn't ask her. I think I subconsciously chose not to believe that of my sister."

"Do you think Robear knew that you were two different people?" I asked.

"I think it's very likely that Robear didn't know," Isobel said. "Giselle could easily have called herself Isobel. Robear paid her call girls in cash, after all, and Robear wouldn't have made the mistake of identifying the body as me if she knew about Giselle."

I sighed. "Rickard and Payton wanted us to think Payton

was dead, because Payton intended to take over Giselle's rich lifestyle, away from the family who could identify her," I said. "And of course, she told Rickard she'd keep him in money to shut him up about her new lifestyle. He thought he had something on her. And he did, until Giselle was cremated, the proof was gone, and Payton killed him."

Werner nodded. "You're right, Mad; it was like the shell game."

I nodded. "Did Payton tell you what she used in those syringes to kill Giselle and Rickard?"

"Insulin, which doesn't show up in a tox screen, because it's already in the bloodstream," Werner said. "What bothers me is that she succeeded, so why come into the open, tonight?"

"She wanted to be rid of us all," Isobel said. "My father and I were about to be lost at sea."

"When did Payton tell you that?" I asked.

"On our way down here, but she was talking crazy like Grand-mère had earlier today," Isobel said, looking pained. "I'm not sure if all this killing wasn't too much for Payton. She was always the emotional one. I thought it was for attention but maybe not."

The medics showed up, and we stood to the side so they could stabilize Isobel.

After they did, they put her on a stretcher and hauled her up the cliff; I monkeyed my way back up, Werner behind me.

"Mad, where's your dress?"

"On a bench up top."

"Nice legs."

I stopped and turned to him. "Maybe you should go ahead of me."

"A gentleman always lets a lady go first."

"Some gentleman."

At the top, Eve threw herself into my arms.

"Did you take good care of my dresses?" I asked.

"Up yours," she snapped.

"That's my feisty girl," Kyle said, squeezing Eve's shoulder.

Eve sobbed and about strangled me with another hug.

Nick took me in his arms after her, and he held tight, and nobody disputed his right to do so. And me, I felt as if I'd come home.

"I can't figure out how the heck Payton expected to get away with this," I said afterward. "It's such a public place."

Nick turned me and pointed toward the river. "There's a yacht waiting not too far distant. Could be kidnapping was the plan. A police boat's on its way out there."

"Oh, you're right. Isobel told us so. I saw a motorboat at the base of the cliffs. Thought it was Cort's. How's Candidate York?"

"He'll pull through," Nick said. "Giselle?"

"Nick, Giselle's been dead for days. That's Payton in the sand. She turned the gun on herself and made a success of *that*, at least."

The party in the Vancortland mansion, up over the rise, seemed to continue. Nobody had come outside to see what was happening, and the music continued to drift down toward the water uninterrupted.

My cell phone rang, and I fished it from Werner's tux pocket.

He looked surprised. "When did you put it in there?"

"When we were dancing. Shh." I listened to my caller and hung up. "Let's go," I said.

"Where?" Werner asked. "I've got a crime scene."

"Meet me at the hospital when you're done, then."

"Are you hurt?" Werner and Nick asked together.

"I'll be on the maternity ward. Sherry's on her way into the delivery room."

Werner looked skeptical.

"When you're there, you can check on Isobel and her father and write your report. As for me, I'm Sherry's backup coach, in case Justin can't go the distance."

I called my dad and Fiona, Brandy and Cort, and Alex and Tricia, while Nick drove us to the hospital in his Hummer.

Sherry was still in labor when I got to the maternity ward while Nick parked the Hummer.

Justin sat in the waiting room, head in his hands. "Ten minutes, and I passed out," he confessed.

I rubbed his arm. "No wonder she wanted a second string."

Justin groaned. "Because I fainted at the ultrasound."

I bit my lip and went in to coach my sister.

By the time the family arrived, and I mean everyone, I was standing beside Sherry's bed in her hospital room showing off babies Kathleen and Reilly Vancortland, a boy and a girl, both named after my mom, her maiden name having been O'Reilly. Mostly I did it because Sherry was exhausted, and I liked holding them.

Sherry and Justin had kept the twin part a secret to surprise us all.

Justin cleared his throat. "Mad, Nick: Sherry and I want you to be Reilly's godparents."

"Of course," I said.

Nick beamed. "You betcha. I'd be honored."

"We're not done," Justin said. "Alex and Tricia, will you be Kathleen's godparents?"

I handed Kathleen to Tricia while Nick and I concentrated on Reilly.

"Hey," Nick said, kissing me on the brow. "We have a boy."

Werner arrived at that moment.

Everyone got quiet.

"Look, Werner," I said. "Nick and I are going to be Reilly's godparents."

He firmed his lips. "Congratulations. Sherry, Justin, congrats to you, too. I'll stop in tomorrow." Werner left.

I looked up at Nick. "Don't go anywhere."

His gaze held mine. "I wouldn't dream of it."

I gave him the baby and ran after Werner. He wouldn't turn, but I caught his arm near the elevator.

"It's okay, Mad," he said. "Nick's practically a member of the Cutler family."

"I wouldn't let my family choose my guy. I chose him a long time ago. I'm sorry that I forgot that for a while."

"I'm not. You're not getting engaged or anything like that, are you?"

"I guess we'll see what time brings."

"Then there's hope."

"Lytton, I haven't been fair to you. You deserve somebody . . . spectacular."

He knuckled my cheek. "You, Madeira Cutler, are spectacular."

"I wish you'd stop being so nice."

"I'm a hard-edged cop, and don't you forget it."

"Yes, sir."

"Go get your guy." He stepped on the elevator, and our gazes held until it closed.

I barely got around the corner to Sherry's hall before I was pulled up against a hard bod. "On again," Nick growled in my ear. "You, me, us. Together."

"Very, very, very on," I said and kissed him.

A cheer rose up from the people spilling out of Sherry's room.

A nurse nearly had a stroke as she shushed them.

My family got shoved back into Sherry's room, and they cheered in whispers when we walked back in.

"Give us our godson," I said, accepting Reilly, while Kelsey raised her arms to Nick. Look at us, I thought, one of each. How right did that feel?

"Well," I said to the room at large, "I know what I have to do."

"What's that?" my father asked.

"I had time to consult with Reilly and Kathleen in the nursery, earlier, and they're both amenable to wearing designer christening outfits. Reilly's will be a tux, of course, and Kathleen's gown will be white and sweet as spun sugar."

"What famous designer makes christening outfits?" Fiona asked.

"Why, Madeira Cutler, of course."

Vintage Bag Tips

I put two of my newest and most favorite vintage bags into this story. One appears on the first morning. Isobel falls for Mad's single-handled, creamy-caramel-swirl-colored Lucite box bag shaped like a man's lunchbox, circa 1950s. It's three and a half inches by six inches deep and four inches high at the curved top. The oval handle stands three inches above that.

Box bags come in Bakelite, Lucite, metal weave, even tortoiseshell. I tested this one to see if it was Lucite or Bakelite. If you wet the plastic with hot running water, and it's Bakelite, it will smell something like formaldehyde. Remember science class? My box bag, I now know, is Lucite.

Box bags are rare and can run into the hundreds of

dollars, especially if they have a name like Wilardy on them. Mine says Made in Hong Kong on a clear plastic strip on the unlined inside. It should have a lining. I would call the hardware functional, not fancy. I bought it for a very reasonable price at Somerville Center Antiques, Somerville, New Jersey. It's a group shop, and I purchased it specifically from Elyse at Kitsch N' Wear. I saw more vintage handbags here than at any antique store I've ever been to. I'd date my caramel box bag as being from the sixties because of the hardware.

The second purse I featured in the story is Maddie's vintage black Ralph Lauren bag. When I found it in a local SAVERS, I practically danced. Engraved on the strap hook and on the strap's upholstery tacks is RLL. It has a Y hook with RLL engraved on the top near the ring holding the strap.

Three fobs hang from the zipper by leather laces that are self-wrapped. Ralph's initials are on one fob in gold, about one and a half inches high. One of the other two fobs is a square of black leather with a gold square on top depicting a stirrup with a horse head on it. The third is a simple stirrup, about two inches high, with Lauren engraved at the bottom.

This bag is made of a black fabric with the designs from all three fobs in differing sizes woven into it. It's zipper-topped, twelve inches square, three inches wide, and the perfect size for my netbook. I'd date this one as coming from the seventies because of its thick, toothy zipper. It was a pure steal.

Look for pictures of these bags and the bags featured in my previous Vintage Magic Mysteries on my website www.annetteblair.com under "Handbags" in the table of contents to the left.

Dear Readers,

In regard to my inspiration for this story: My neighbors are identical triplets who inspired me to write my psychic triplet witch series for Berkley Sensation. I engaged one in conversation outside last summer, and she straightened from washing her car and said, "You think I'm one of the triplets, don't you?"

Of course I did, but no, she's their first cousin. I couldn't tell them apart.

In Skirting the Grave, *I made the parents of the "dead ringers" twin sisters married to the York brothers for added plausibility. My mother and her sister married brothers, and I defy you to sort the six of us into two correct sets. I connected the dots between the two situations, and this story was born.*

—Annette Blair

Turn the page for a preview of
Annette Blair's next book
in the Vintage Magic Mysteries . . .

Cloaked in Malice

Coming soon from Berkley Prime Crime!

My name is Madeira Cutler, and I'd like to invent a
ghostly tracking device. I mean, there's nothing like a
dead person dropping into your personal space to set you
up for the day. Or to knock you off your Jimmy Choos.

"Dante, you scared the wits out of me," I said, my
heart racing.

"My apologies," said my dapper Cary Grant clone in
tux tails and top hat, "but I just saw a ghost."

"You *are* a ghost."

"Semantics." He had the wisdom to put some distance between us. "Why so scared?" he asked. "You're
used to having me around. I introduced myself before
you moved into my eternal restless place."

I smoothed and folded the Hermès scarf I'd crushed

in my hand at the minor fright. "It's a Saturday, the shop's barely open, and the residents of Mystic have the good grace to sleep in. And I was alone, sorting vintage clothes, and thinking about—"

"Nick?"

"Shush. Maybe. And suddenly I have a heart-shocking face-to-face. I'm here to tell you, being startled in that particular way can scare a girl."

"My apologies, but seriously, *you* put your designer vintage dress shop in a former funeral home carriage house—horse-drawn hearses, caskets, old embalming room, and all."

"Wait, this isn't about me," I said. "It's about you being freaked by a ghost. Surely Mr. Undertaker Under-hill, you've seen your share?"

"Not like this one."

My shop bell rang, and a curly-haired young blonde entered, fashionably attired in vintage seventies, a stranger, with the most unique baby blues I'd ever seen—well, no, I had seen eyes like hers before.

I shivered deep inside, and Chakra, my cat, catapulted into my arms to soothe me. "Welcome to Vintage Magic," I said, stroking Chakra's caramel-swirl fur coat.

She turned a full 360, like a little girl in a candy store. "I'll take one of everything." She about swooned over my vintage treasures. By the twinkle and excitement in her eyes, I could see that she loved the possibilities.

"This place is wonderful, just brimming over with—

Oh, look, you have street signs. Mad as a Hatter, Little Black Dress Lane, Paris when it Sizzles." She chuckled and turned back to us—I mean, she turned back to *me*, though Dante remained beside me, his wide-eyed gaze glued to her.

"What do you think?" he asked me. "Is she a dead ringer or what?"

I wanted to shush him. It's difficult to carry on a conversation with a ghost and a live person at the same time. No, my customer couldn't hear or see the hunk in his work clothes. And yes, Dante died of a heart attack during a funeral. Go figure. Evidently, one wears for eternity what one dies wearing.

Dolly Sweet, aged one hundred three and three-quarters, planned to die in her Katharine Hepburn gown, the one like the wedding gown in *The Philadelphia Story*. So of course I had heart palpitations every time she wore it.

No one could see Dante but me, my Aunt Fiona—not really my aunt, but really a witch—nuff said—and Dolly.

Why Dolly? Because she'd had an illicit affair with Dante more than half a century ago. Arguably, Mystic's biggest secret. Their love had transcended time, as had the gossip.

Dolly had been young, beautiful, unmarried and, shall we say, unsullied? Dante, renowned rake, was, and still is, drop-dead gorgeous—the Cary Grant description is not an exaggeration. He'd been at least fifteen, if not twenty, years her senior at the time, and the last living heir to the wealthiest dynasty in Mystic, Connecticut.

The gossip might have gone down in history as speculation, if not for the fact that when Dante died, he left Dolly everything, this building included, which she sold to me for the cost of taxes. I love them both dearly, and I love that they're still attracted to each other, he a debonair fifty-year-old ghost; she a wrinkled centenarian in the prime of her life. Even now, they dallied, every chance they got, in their favorite of my nooks: Paris, making it more of an inferno than a sizzle.

So why could Dante not take his gaze from the young stranger facing us?

I extended my hand. "I'm Madeira, call me Maddie, Cutler, and this is my shop."

"Nice to meet you." Her grip was firm, eye contact on target, nothing to hide. "Paisley Skye. Sounds fake, doesn't it?"

"Not at all," I said, taken by surprise. Frankly, though her question was jarring, the image was inspirational.

The bell above the door jingled, again, and Dolly Sweet and her daughter-in-law, Ethel, came in. They were regulars and very early risers, no matter what day of the week. I'd often counted on them for an early homemade breakfast full of love and friendly chatter.

Dolly's eyes brightened when she spotted Dante behind the counter.

"Look at Mad's customer, Doll," Dante said, "and tell me she doesn't remind you of someone."

I wanted to remind Dante that only Dolly and I could hear him. "Dolly," I said. "This is Paisley. Paisley, this is Dolly and her daughter-in-law, Ethel."

"Hello, Dolly," Paisley said, her abbreviated laugh in perfect sync with Dolly's, in tone and cadence, at least. Their voices sounded nothing alike.

Dolly tilted her head. "Ethel," she said, "does she remind you of me when I was young?"

"Well, I don't know, Mama. You looked seventy when I married your son."

"I was fifty-six."

"Same difference." Ethel turned to Paisley. "We used to think fifty was old. But Dolly, now, she's officially old . . . as dirt."

"Thank you, dear."

Dante chuckled, charming the cherries off Dolly's straw hat.

Paisley's smile, beside Dolly's, those unique eyes—periwinkle blue, if I didn't miss my guess—sure did it for me. "You know, you two do look like you could be distantly related."

The hand Paisley raised to her temple trembled. "You know, I've dreamed all my life of hearing somebody say that."

A new Needlecraft Mystery from *USA Today* bestselling author

MONICA FERRIS

Buttons and Bones

❈ ❈ ❈

Owner of the Crewel World needlework shop and part-time sleuth Betsy Devonshire heads with friends for the Minnesota north woods to renovate an old cabin. But beneath the awful linoleum is something even uglier—a human skeleton. Betsy's investigation leads her to the site of a former German POW camp, a mysterious cro-cheted rug, and an intricately designed pattern of clues to a decades-old crime.

penguin.com